# Face the Lion

# Face the Lion

## Mark Marchetti

*This is a work of historical fiction.*
*Some historical characters and events are real...*
*while others are borrowed, combined,*
*or completely imagined.*
*All non-historical characters portrayed in this novel are*
*entirely fictitious,*
*and any similarity to actual persons, living or dead, is*
*entirely coincidental.*

*For Jim and Joan.*
*Your love and dedication to each other*
*has been an inspiration to*
*your family and friends.*

# Contents

# Introduction

In every culture there are rituals and practices considered to be 'rites of passage' into adulthood. These 'rites of passage' can carry multiple rituals leading up to the event or in our modern world simply be attached to an age the individual has achieved. In what the western world would consider third world tribal communities the young man or woman must often be tested... face a challenge or fear and overcome it to be considered an adult. Some of the rituals or practices we would view as torturous or barbaric. Our legalistic approach seems to center around becoming a 'legal adult'... reaching an age where the person is expected to be competent to take on adult responsibilities whether they are ready for it or not. The legal age for drinking, smoking, driving a car, getting married are all western world inventions. They are milestones in a life where nothing is measured or tested other than longevity.

As any of us who have lived a bit know, it takes much more than the ability to live a desired number of years to be socially or legally able to take on adult responsibilities. It takes some longer to reach that point, while some never will. Sometimes, as in the case of Marlin Colby, it takes a traumatic event in his life to force him to move on into adulthood... force him to face his fears. Marlin's adventure will take him away from his privileged life in Charleston, S.C. onto the sea as a sailor, and finally to Africa, retracing and learning about the life of a father he barely knew.

There can be no place in the world more different than Africa in comparison to Marlin's life in Charleston. A country pillaged by foreign interests for centuries, in Africa, Marlin will learn life lessons and why his father was so drawn to the rawness of life there.

## Chapter 1

# Right Of Passage

In the African plains Sironka lay on the floor of his darkened hut staring at the ceiling. He could smell the grasses of the savanna that surrounded the village and had slept very little over the long night. His thoughts were of what lay ahead of him in the morning. All the ritual ceremonies had been completed and in the morning he would have to face his fears to become a man... but more importantly he would become a warrior. From his earliest point of memory this is what he had aspired to become; it was the center of his desire and the focus of his young life. Now he was on the verge of reaching his goal... provided he survived.

From the beginning of time there has always been a warrior class… men who were either thrust into the role by necessity or possibly enslaved into the role of soldier by a monarch. These were the men who were content as farmers or herders but were forced to take up arms. There has always been a class of men who actively sought out the role of a warrior. They stood apart from the others and were seen as the protectors of the society or culture. In some cultures, like the Maasai, it was an expected and desired goal of all young men.

In Sironka's tribe there was no person more respected or honored than the warrior. Life in the African plains was always on the edge. Little water, often little food and surrounded by wild animals that would consider you an easy meal, the tribal warriors were the hunters and the protectors. They were the men who stood between the everyday dangers facing the tribe's survival and protected their most prized possession, the livestock, but to become a warrior they would first have to pass a test. Now the age old drama was again about to play out.

The air was cool and the stars still visible as the sun rose in the East over the far away Mt. Kilimanjaro. The African heat would soon take over but for the moment Sironka just stood in the cool morning air and looked over his village. He had never been more than twenty miles from the village in his entire short life. The village was his world… all he knew and all he cared about. He would leave alone this morning to hunt a lion. If he was successful he would come back to the village as a man and a warrior. If he was not, this would be the last time he would see his village. If he were to run as a coward, everyone would know and he would face that shame every day for the rest of his life. The chances were if he ran the lion would kill him and he would never face the shame. Even at his young age, death was more preferable than life as a coward. He left the village alone that morning with his razor sharp spear and a small hide covered shield.

Sironka knew where he was going and where his lion would be. He had been scouting, stalking and watching him for two weeks. There was no shortage of lions on the African plains, but the male he was looking for was distinctive. He had a black mane and like most males would not be amongst the females of the pride, but some distance away. He knew that when lions weren't hunting or eating, they were sleeping and since most of the hunting was done by the females, the male lion slept most of the day. The male lion was the warrior of his clan much the same as the warriors of Sironka's village. At night the male would patrol his territory, marking it as he moved. If the scent marker wasn't enough, he would periodically let out a loud roar to warn any would be rivals. While the females were deadly in their own right, it was the male lion that watched over and protected his harem. It was their job to hunt and his job to protect and sire more lions... not that he wasn't fully capable of killing when he needed to. To prove himself a man and worthy of warrior status, Sironka would have to kill a male lion. Female lions or an old or sick lion was not acceptable... it must be a healthy, strong male lion. This was not his first lion hunt. He had been allowed to go on hunts with warriors as an observer when they hunted in a group but to prove his worthiness, he would now have to hunt the lion alone. A healthy male lion could weigh up to five hundred fifty pounds with four inch teeth and three inch claws...

the supreme predator of the savanna, designed to tear apart its prey quickly and efficiently... a fact Sironka knew and respected.

Sironka knew what he would have to do. He would have to get close enough to the lion to plunge his spear into its body to make the kill. If the lion were to run from him and he threw his spear he might be alright but if the lion charged, he knew he must not throw the spear. If he threw the spear and missed, he would surely die... the lion would be on him and tear him apart in a split second. Sironka was well aware of his chances of success having seen a number of young men go on the hunt to never return. His shield would be useless in an attack of that kind and was ceremonial at best. His plan was to approach the sleeping lion from downwind to hide his scent. Before he made his approach he would coat his body with a mixture of mud and grass to further hide his scent, then he would slowly and very carefully sneak up on the sleeping lion. Lions have an excellent sense of smell. On some occasions the lion would get the scent of the hunter and run but Sironka had studied his lion carefully. He believed the lion he was hunting would not run, he would stand and fight. To insure this he knew he would have to make the lion mad, make him feel threatened, corner him to test his bravery. He wanted his lion to charge so he could use the lion's weight and momentum against him.

Sironka moved carefully into the plains towards where he knew the lions would be waiting. When he found them he made sure he was downwind and found a place to watch from until he could locate the male with the dark mane. The lions were fat from feasting on an overnight kill and several of the females were cleaning the blood from their faces. Soon they would lie down and sleep.

As he suspected the male was moving away from the females and into a brush area out of view where he could sleep undisturbed under an Acacia tree. Sironka took some water from his goat bag and mixed some mud with the dry dirt, spreading it all over his body. He took a long, last drink of water and left his shield and water bag behind as he began the hunt. He felt no fear, only determination… he would kill the lion or be killed in the process. He would not be a coward. He would be a warrior.

Slowly and carefully Sironka crawled through the high tan colored grass towards where the lion was sleeping. The grass still had some morning dew and had a fresh smell to it. He was constantly aware of the wind direction and the position of the females. If the females caught his scent and became aware of his presence they might come looking for him. If that were the case the male would be alerted and the tables would be turned… the lions would be hunting him. They would blend into the grass and could be unseen. Sironka was well aware of his surroundings and had studied with the hunters of his tribe. He knew the wind patterns and how they would change as the sun moved higher in the sky and warmed the air. He had a limited amount of time to get to his target before the lions would pick up his scent and he would become the target.

He slowly moved forward in the tall grass constantly checking his position. Then he stopped and froze in place. Directly in front of him was an Egyptian cobra. The snake seemed docile and non-aggressive, but as one of the deadliest snakes in the world he had to respect it. He pushed his spear towards the snake not with the intent to kill it but to get it to move along so he could proceed. His heart was beating fast and for the first time fear started to take hold. One quick bite from the snake and his life would be over. These snakes are known to be very aggressive if cornered and if he were to find himself battling the snake, the lions would quickly know he was there. He hoped that since the snake wasn't cornered it would just move away. He gently poked at the snake with the spear and the snake quickly took a defensive position, rising to face Sironka, sounding an evil hiss with its distinctive hood spread. The standoff seemed to last forever in Sironka's mind but was in actuality only a few moments. Then the snake quickly moved away into the safety of the bush and the hunt continued.

He had moved close to the lion now and could smell musty scent of the lion as the breeze touched his face. He could hear its breathing and could see it sheltered in the brush under the Acacia tree, his dark black mane shining in the morning sun. He was lying against a large log comfortably stretched out, confident that no other creature would dare to disturb him. As Sironka got into position he could feel the wind direction start to change. Soon his scent would carry to the lion and he would become aware of his presence but Sironka wasn't close enough yet. He crawled closer and the closer he crawled the larger the lion became. He knew there was no going back now. If he jumped and ran the lion would chase him down. If the male didn't get him, the lionesses, who were not too far away would quickly view him as a threat and chase him down. For an instant the fear crept in but like a true warrior, fear of being a coward was greater than the fear of death, and fear, like the lion, needed to be conquered so he continued to move forward. The wind had now shifted and he could see the lion's nose sniffing for scent.

The lion now started to awake from his slumber knowing something was not right and Sironka knew this was his time to act. All he had dreamed of... all he had aspired to become was within his grasp. The lion started to rise up searching the air for the scent of his hunter. Sironka stood up holding his spear with both hands as the lion now became aware of his presence. The lion jumped up quickly now... more quickly than Sironka was ready for and faced off his hunter. The lion was not cornered as Sironka had wanted and could have run away in the blink of an eye, but not this lion. He looked directly at Sironka his yellow eyes filled with rage and growled... a low, prime evil growl putting a deep fear into Sironka, the type of fear all prey animals must feel in that last instant before they are killed, torn to pieces and consumed. The lion was not intimidated or afraid... the lion felt his territory had been encroached on and he wasn't going to stand for it.

The lion dug his rear paws into the dirt like a sprinter preparing to start a race. In a splint second the lion was charging towards him, his eyes locked on his would be assassin, determined to kill him. Every fiber in his body told him to run, but Sironka stood his ground. As the lion lunged towards him, he plunged the razor sharp spear deep into the lion's body. The forward momentum and the weight of the beast pushed the spear deep into his heart. The lion swiped at Sironka with his claws slashing him across his chest before it landed on top of him. The lion was mortally wounded but it took a few minutes to bleed out and die, all the while struggling to hold onto life and trying to kill his attacker. Sironka was able to stay clear to the teeth and claws until death came. When it was over, he was able to crawl out from under the huge lion, now covered in the lion's blood, and as he stood over the giant cat, he let out a scream of victory... a scream of conquest, adrenaline, and relief.

He quickly looked around to see where the other lions were while pulling the spear from the lion's body and could not see them. The females fled with their young to safety, startled by what had happened. While his wounds were bleeding, they weren't life threatening and would become scars he would wear as a badge of honor for his entire life. He was now a warrior. Covered in the blood of the lion along with his own blood, he was now surrounded by his brother warriors ready to help retrieve his prize.

They would take the mane and give it to the women of the tribe who would braid it and make it into a head dress that Sironka would wear on special occasions. The tail would be stretched and softened to become a flag to be flown over the Manyatta (warrior's camp). The lion's teeth would be given to the women and children to make necklaces. Sironka's journey to become a man had been completed... but his journey as a man was just starting. Many years after the killing of the lion his path would cross another's... a young man on a quest to discover how to become a man in a different world, a world much different from Sironka's.

*Chapter 2*

# Mary

On the outskirts of Charleston, South Carolina, Mary Luzzetti lay in her bed, the moonlight streaming through the windows of her room. She stared at the ceiling and listened, alert to any sound that might indicate any of her family were still awake... especially her father. She was both scared and excited, thinking about what she was about to do. It was almost eleven o'clock before she dared to slip from under her covers and get out of bed. She quietly got dressed in the moonlight and then removed a small suitcase from its hiding place under her bed. She left an envelope with a note on her nightstand and then very carefully opened the door to her room. She listened for a moment before picking up the suitcase and moving into the hallway. Carefully she closed the door to her room and then slowly moved down the staircase in bare feet so she would make no noise. She had to pass her parents room before making it to the staircase. Almost unable to breathe, she could feel her heart pounding in her chest.

When she reached the bottom of the stairs she looked back up and felt a slight bit of relief... all was still quiet. She moved from the base of the stairs, through the kitchen, to the back door of the house. Carefully she opened the door and it made a slight squeaking noise. The noise was barely audible but in her heightened state of awareness it sounded like church bells being rung. She quickly slipped out the door with her suitcase and moved down the stairs, off the porch. She slipped on her shoes and started to walk away quickly from the house towards the road at the edge of the woods. She looked back towards the house several times expecting at any moment to see the lights come on and hear her father yelling after her.

Just off the roadway, tucked into the woods waited a young man in a two tone blue 1928 Ford Sedan. He had been there for the last hour waiting under the trees hanging thick with Spanish moss. The windows of the car were open and the air was warm and still. The sounds of the night; croaking frogs and cricket chirps were all that could be heard. The moon was bright allowing him to see into the night. The longer he sat there in the car, the more certain he was that at any minute the girl's father would spring upon him... maybe even shoot him for trying to steal his daughter away.

The longer he sat, the more nervous he became as the shadows played tricks on his eyes. He tried to think only good thoughts… how they first met… how much he loved her. It was at a dance where they were introduced by a friend. She was quiet and shy, not dressed in a fancy dress as most of the other girls, but she was absolutely beautiful. She seemed out of place at a dance where most of the young people were from fairly wealthy families. He found out a girl friend of hers brought her as a guest and her family was not wealthy, just an average working class family trying to live through an era of economic depression in 1930.

He began to see her on a regular basis, much to the regret of his family that viewed the relationship as ill suited. It was the same for her family. Her parents, especially her father, disapproved of the relationship. His family felt he should socialize with people from his own social class… people with money and power. Her father wanted her to marry within her own Italian culture, not into an Irish family. While both families did as much as they could to keep them apart they still would see each other whenever they could, finally determining the only way they could be together would be if they ran away and were married. So they found themselves in the middle of the night getting ready to elope.

He saw a shadow approaching towards his car and he felt a sense of fear until he realized it was her. He quickly got out of the car as she approached and she ran into his arms. They kissed and then quickly released their embrace realizing where they were and what they were in the process of doing.

He picked up her suitcase and asked, "You okay?"

"Yes," she answered. "But we better get out of here."

She got into the front passenger seat and he put the suitcase in the back seat of the car. He quickly got behind the wheel, started the car and carefully pulled out of the hiding spot turning the car south onto the roadway. Soon Charleston would be far behind them.

He looked over at her and could see there was anticipation on her face. "You scared?" he asked.

"A little… more just excited than scared."

He tried to reassure her. "It'll be okay. You'll see. We'll get to Florida and we can get married… our parents will come around… you'll see."

Marlin Colby and Mary Luzzetti had started their life together… he was just nineteen and she was seventeen. The world might view them as impossibly mismatched but they saw it differently. They viewed the world in the simple terms of two young people in love, doing what they felt they had to do in order to be together. His family was wealthy, having a variety of holdings that had made them immune from the depression. Of course they had been affected, but Marlin's late father had diversified his holdings many years before his death and the family fortune had been protected. Their wealth made them among the elite of Charleston society, even if they were Irish Catholics. Mary's family was getting by but it was a struggle. Her father was a skilled laborer but as an immigrant, English was a second language to him and staying employed was sometimes a problem. He was a proud, honest man, who worked hard. He was also a realistic man who could not see his daughter involved with a man in a different social class and different background than his own. He could believe in a better life for himself and his family in America but could not envision the dream of his daughter.

The car continued down the road into the darkness. After a time they crossed the state line into Georgia and later into Florida. Marlin had figured they could find someone to marry them down in the Keys. He had heard about the Florida Keys from some of the sailors on his father's ships. There was a bit of an outlaw quality to the Keys and he had heard that things down there were less strict... less questions would be asked. Mary had left a note for her parents explaining that they were leaving to be married, taking care not to mention where they were going. Marlin had enough money with him so they could get married and stay away for a several weeks before they went back. They believed after a few weeks had passed they could face the music of both the families and it would be too late for them to do anything about it.

Mary was asleep in the seat next to Marlin. Occasionally, he would glance over for an instant just to admire her. He was a good driver and wasn't speeding or taking any chances. He figured it would be her family notifying the authorities when they found the note and realized she was gone but that wouldn't be until morning. They would notify the authorities, and the authorities would notify his mother and step-father. It wouldn't be a pretty scene but at least they had no idea which way they went.

They were about ten miles out of St. Augustine on a small two lane road when suddenly there was a bright glare of headlights directly in front of the car. Marlin was blinded and swerved to keep from being struck head on. The driver of the oncoming truck was partly tired and but mostly drunk when he drifted over the line.

The truck side swiped Marlin's car and he flew off the road surface. The car slid as Mary awoke from her sleep seeing they were out of control. The last thing Marlin heard before the sound of the crash was the sound of Mary's scream. The car had hit a tree and Mary had been killed instantly. Her small body crushed in the wreckage showed little visible damage, almost like she could have opened her eyes, got up, and walked away. The reality was the life had been crushed from her. Marlin had been knocked out and had a cut on his forehead which was bleeding profusely.

Sam Wiggins had been driving the truck and would have fled the scene except that his truck had a flat tire. He had been drinking and was half asleep at the wheel when the accident occurred. He went over to Marlin's car and looked over the scene. He checked Mary's pulse and found none. He could see that Marlin was still alive and so he checked him out more closely. He found his wallet and took the money then put the wallet back in his pocket. He knew he couldn't leave the scene and knew he had to make it look to be Marlin's fault. It wouldn't be too long before the sun would be up and someone would be driving down the road. Sam went back to his truck and found his bottle of whiskey, then returned to Marlin's car. He took the whiskey and poured some on Marlin to make sure when the authorities arrived they would be able to smell it. Then he checked on the unconscious Marlin and attempted to pour some whiskey down his throat. He choked as a reflex, unable to swallow the whiskey and he remained unconscious. The stage now set, Sam Wiggins waited for someone to drive upon the scene so he could flag them down for help.

Just as the sun came up an old truck came down the road and Sam flagged it down. Sam took the driver over to the wreck in part to show him he needed help and in part to get his story out. "The girl's dead far as I can tell," he pointed out. "Don't know how bad the boy's hurt... knocked out but bleedin' pretty good."

The driver of the old truck checked on Mary and could see that all the color had left her face. "What a shame, such a pretty young thing," he stated in a sad, almost reverent tone. "The boy is alive, but he don't look good... I best get movin' an' get some help." That didn't satisfy Sam Wiggins; he needed to get more of his story out.

"It happened real fast ya know... he just come over the line an' side swiped my truck. I think he musta been drunk... I could smell booze on him. What do you think? Could you smell it?"

The driver of the old truck didn't answer, seeming more intent on going to get some help. "I'll send help back soon as I can," he yelled back at Sam as he got back in his truck and headed towards St. Augustine.

## Chapter 3

# St. Augustine

An ambulance and police car arrived on scene and the investigation begun. It was officially determined that Mary was dead at the scene and Marlin was removed from the vehicle still unconscious and transported to a hospital. It was some time before he started to regain consciousness. When he opened his eyes his vision was blurred and things took time to come into focus. The first person he saw was a nurse in a white uniform looking down at him.

"Where am I?" he asked in a soft confused voice. "Mary… where's Mary?"

"Doctor... doctor... he's waking up," the nurse announced as she stepped back from the bed.

Marlin's first instinct was to start to sit up and get his bearings, but he found himself unable to do so. His head started to spin and he had to lie down again. The doctor came over to him and started to look him over. "Don't try to move son. You've had a bad blow to the head; you need to just lie still for a while."

"What happened... where's Mary?" Marlin asked in a dazed voice. The doctor looked at the young man and simply replied, "Don't worry about her now, just rest."

The nurse looked at the doctor knowing full well that the girl was dead. "Why didn't you tell him?" she whispered in a judgmental tone. "Why didn't you tell him his girlfriend is dead?"

The doctor sensed what the nurse was getting at. She believed Marlin had been responsible for the girls' death. When he was brought in there was an unmistakable odor of liquor on him. She made the assumption just as Sam Wiggins had wanted... the assumption that the accident had been Marlin's fault because he was drunk.

The doctor was a middle aged man with a good deal of worldly as well as medical experience. He looked over at the nurse and simply stated, "It's my job... as well as yours, to help the living. There's nothing I can do for that poor young girl. Telling him that kind of news right now won't do him any good... might be worse for him. Things are not always as they may appear."

The nurse knew she was being scolded in the doctor's own way but the doctor wasn't convinced she was getting the message. He looked directly at her and stated, "And I don't want you or any of the other staff telling him of the girl's death... his people will be here soon and the Sheriff is handling those matters... do I make myself clear nurse!"

Now she got the message loud and clear, responding in a short, "Yes Doctor."

Marlin had received a severe concussion and was in and out of consciousness for the remainder of the day. Back home, the news of the accident had reached both families. As Marlin had predicted, Mary's father went to the police to report his daughter had been kidnapped. After reading the note, the desk sergeant explained to him that she had run away to be married. The difference in the distinctions did not make the issue any better in her father's mind. It wasn't long after reporting her missing the authorities received the news of the accident and her death. An officer was sent to the small home to deliver the sad news. In the short span of only a few hours Mary's family went through the emotional range of anger and confusion over her running away to the overwhelming grief of never seeing her alive again.

At Marlin's home, the news was received differently. A ranking officer from the police department was sent to Marlin's home. When he arrived he was greeted by a butler and then escorted into the study where he was announced to George Reilly, Marlin's step-father.

"Mr. Reilly, I am Captain Jones from the police department..." he announced.

"Yes, I can see that," Reilly responded in a short tone. "What can I do for you?"

"It's about your son, sir... Marlin."

"You mean my step son, Captain. Yes, what about him?" he asked in a tone making sure the family relationship was noted.

"He's been in an accident sir... near St. Augustine... in Florida."

"Florida! There must be some mistake... he's not in Florida. Calvin! Get in here!" he hollered.

Calvin, the butler, came into the room quickly, "Yes sir, Mister Reilly."

"Go up to Marlin's room and get him down here."

The Captain began to explain the situation. "We got a call from the Sheriff in St. Augustine about a car accident involving Marlin and a girl... Mary Luzzetti."

Before he could continue, Calvin quickly came back in the room. "He ain't in his room sir, but I found this here letter." He gave the letter to George Reilly who quickly opened it and read it as an angry look came over his face. He gathered his composure and looked back at the Police Captain.

"Go on... explain the situation," he calmly stated.

The Captain gave Reilly the details including the death of Mary Luzzetti. He included the information from the Sheriff's department that there was reason to believe the accident was caused by drunk driving. Reilly took down all the information, thanked the Captain for his service, and then slipped some money into his hand, treating him as he would a delivery boy as he escorted him to the door. After the Captain was gone, George Reilly went into the study again and called the family lawyer, Sean Kilgore, instructing him to immediately come to the home. Now it was time to gather the family and tell them of the incident.

George Reilly married Marlin's mother when Martin was about twelve and his sister was about sixteen. His father had died when Marlin was eleven. Marlin's father, Robert Colby, was a jovial man, generous with his family, friends, and employees. He did have his serious, business side, and had become extremely successful. He knew how he was viewed by the established, wealthy, families of Charleston and didn't care. He was viewed as an Irish upstart who had more luck than brains. He knew differently. He was a good businessman and smiled every time he out smarted them or put them in a position where they were forced to deal with him. He would tell his close associates to always smile... just kill them with kindness... in the end we always win! Over the years, with a touch of reluctance, the other upscale families began to accept the Colby's, in part because they had to.

George Reilly had done some business with Marlin's father and when he died he saw an opportunity to ingratiate himself to a wealthy widow. He was a greedy man but polished in the social graces. He called on the family frequently attempting to win favor. Soon he was offering advice and the courtship began. Marlin's mother retained control of all the family holdings and while she was lonely and in need of attention, she wasn't a fool. George was smooth and in the end he won her over. George was kind to Marlin and his sister... at first. He knew that to gain the favor of the mother he would have to be attentive to the children. Marlin was never able to warm up to George... there was just something about him he didn't like, though he was polite for his mother's sake. Marlin and George were distinctly different in almost every way. Marlin was a quiet, thoughtful introvert... a bit shy and awkward.

George hid his deceitful, rough, bullying nature under the polished gentleman image he projected. Eventually, he was able to convince Marlin's mother to marry and she believed at the time he would be a good step father to her two children. Things didn't go exactly as Ruth Colby or George Reilly had planned.

During that era, it wasn't considered good form or acceptable for a woman to run a business, especially a large enterprise such as the Colby's. Before his passing, Marlin's father made it clear his wealth would be passed to his wife and she would be the person to control it with the help of a longtime friend, the family attorney. Provisions had been made so she would not be able to transfer wealth or control of it to a second husband, in time it would pass to Marlin and his sister. He knew she would be a target for men like George Reilly if something were to happen to him. George Reilly expected he would have access to the wealth and would be running the show but found out differently. True to her first husband's wishes, Ruth Colby, ran the businesses and made the decisions with the help of the attorney. At first she would listen and consult George for his advice, but later the as the marriage soured she no longer sought his advice. George was allowed to be viewed as the head of the firm, even given that title, but was not given control of the money. He was paid a very lucrative salary for his service… much more than he could have ever made on his own and much more than he was worth. It was still in his best interest that all the company holdings did well but the control he wanted he never could obtain. Over the years Reilly had tried to bribe and corrupt the family attorney without success. His relationship with Ruth had been strained due to his philandering ways and they remained married only because of her strict Catholic upbringing and his need of money. Ruth knew she had made a bad choice in her second marriage but continued to stay the course. Marlin's sister had few dealings with him and held no particular contempt but Marlin had no use for him. Marlin had been very close to his father and grew to have a strong dislike for George. The feeling was mutual with George and he disliked Marlin.

George was a large bully of a man who took great pleasure in his physical intimidation of Marlin. He took every opportunity to abuse and humiliate him. He knew Marlin was afraid of him, to the point of cowering in his presence, and was the most vocal in his displeasure about him seeing Mary. Much of his abuse towards Marlin was subtle but very effective. He knew that any overt physical abuse his wife would never stand for so he was careful. He might push Marlin around a little, call him names to belittle him or make threats if Ruth were not around. When she was around George displayed ambivalence towards Marlin but the tension between them was thick.

George Reilly was conflicted. On one level he saw the opportunity to get rid of Marlin. He could see him being sent off to jail for a while… less conflict in the home, maybe a better chance with Ruth to gain access to more money. He could also see the same possibilities if he were to help Marlin out of the problem… he would owe him and Ruth would be pleased. He could also see that a scandal would tarnish the family reputation and that might be a problem for him. He made the decision to take the role of compassionate step father thinking it would be in his best interest and his best interest was his only consideration.

When the attorney, Sean Kilgore, arrived Reilly explained the situation before gathering the family. He wanted to be certain that Kilgore knew what he wanted done before Ruth arrived downstairs.

"Sean," he began. "I want you to go down to St. Augustine as soon as possible. I need you to arrive there before I arrive with Ruth... this could be very hard on her. See what the situation is and who is in charge... who we need to pay off to make this matter go away."

Sean Kilgore never let on his dislike for Reilly and over the years his loyalty was always to Ruth first so he just let on that he was willing and able to proceed with Reilly's plan... to a point. He heard him out and knew that in the real world many things would go away when the proper people were paid off. In the business dealings of the time it was a common accepted practice but this might be different. "Keep in mind George; this may be more complicated than you think. Remember a girl was killed in this accident," he explained.

"Damn it Sean... I know the little bitch was killed, but she was just a tramp from the other side of the tracks... the foolish fancy of a foolish boy... I must protect Ruth," Reilly stated in a tone of contempt for Mary and compassion for Ruth. "We need to keep the matter out of the papers as much as possible... payoff who we have to... make it disappear as much as possible."

Kilgore agreed but knew better than to trust or believe his sympathetic tone. Compassion, especially towards Marlin, was not in his nature. He was just trying to figure what his angle was when Ruth and Marlin's sister, Alice, entered the study. Ruth was surprised to see Sean Kilgore when she entered. "Oh Sean!" she exclaimed. "What brings you to our home so early in the morning?"

Reilly interrupted, "I called him dear… there's been an accident, I thought it best he come over… you better sit down."

Ruth Colby Reilly was not a frail or feeble minded woman. She was an attractive woman with style and class, quite capable of making hard decisions. George preferred to treat her as a person who needed his masculine strength and she played along knowing full well she was fully in charge. She sat down and motioned for Alice to do the same. "Go on George, explain what's going on."

"It's Marlin," he started.

"Marlin!" she gasped. "What's happened? Where is he?"

"He's alive and being cared for. He's in the Flagler Hospital in St. Augustine," Reilly announced in a tone of importance and command.

"St. Augustine…" she said sounding puzzled.

He went on to explain how Marlin and Mary Luzzetti were in the process of eloping, the car crash, and Mary's death. He explained where Marlin was and that he was sending Kilgore to St. Augustine to see what needed to be done. As he explained the facts, Alice began to cry at the thought of Mary dying in the car. She liked Mary and had always thought the romance between her brother and Mary was the stuff of dreams.

Ruth too was thinking of the young girl. While she didn't favor her as the girl her son should marry she didn't dislike her. At that moment she could only think of how her parents must feel… the pain… the loss. "Her poor parents, this must be horrible for them."

"Yes, I'm sure it is," Reilly interjected somewhat coldly. "But right now we must think of Marlin… what's best for him. I believe we should go to St. Augustine as soon as possible."

With the meeting was over, the family went to pack some bags for the trip to St. Augustine and Sean Kilgore left to do the same. Reilly would delay the family leaving to give enough time for Kilgore to arrive and get the information he wanted.

*Chapter 4*

# Confuse the issue

Marlin lay in his hospital bed still stunned and confused, unable to think properly. The Sheriff was talking with the doctor to see if he could question him about the accident. A death was involved and there would surely be an inquest to seek the cause. Sheriff Jacob Monroe was in charge and had by this time learned the identity of Marlin and who his family was.

"Doctor, I need to talk with that boy," the Sheriff insisted. "I need to get a statement from him... you know, see what happened out there."

The doctor was firm with the Sheriff, "Jacob, I know what you need to do, but that boy isn't in any condition to be talkin' to you yet. He's had a bad blow to the head an' it will take some time before he can talk to you. I don't believe right now he even knows how he got here or what happened."

"Tell me this at least," the Sheriff prodded. "Was he drunk? My deputy tells me he smelled booze on the boy... is that a fact?"

"I can only tell you this," the doctor replied. "We did smell booze on him when he came in, but once we removed his clothes and cleaned him up we didn't smell it any more. If he was drunk... as drunk as you suspect, we would have still smelled it on his breath. His reactions were of a man with a concussion, not of a man who was drunk... that's all I can tell you."

The Sheriff frowned as he reluctantly left advising the doctor, "I'll check back with you later."

The doctor had his doubts about Marlin being drunk at the time of the accident. He had seen enough drunks in the hospital to know when someone was clearly under the influence of alcohol but the matter was out of his hands. All he could do is present the facts as he saw them.

When Sean Kilgore arrived at the hospital he met with the doctor and was given the same information as the Sheriff. He went to see Marlin who was a little more coherent by that time. Marlin told him all he remembered; the lights in his eyes, sliding off the roadway, and hearing Mary's scream. Sean broke the news to Marlin that Mary was dead and the boy completely broke down, crying hysterically. Sean knew Marlin since the day he started to work for his father as a young talented attorney directly out of law school.

The boy's grief and anguish touched him deeply and he comforted him as best he could before leaving the room. Before leaving he instructed Marlin to make no statement to anyone about the accident until he returned to see him, then he spoke with the doctor.

"Doctor, I'm afraid I upset Marlin a great deal… I had to break the news to him about Mary and he's taking it very hard."

"I understand," the doctor answered. "We had waited until a family member would arrive… thinking that would be best. I'll give him something to calm him a bit."

Sean Kilgore was an excellent attorney as well as a family friend and his primary goal at that point was to protect Marlin. "I would appreciate that Marlin not be questioned or disturbed until he is in a better mental state. I think you would agree that he is not in any condition to be questioned by anyone at this time. As his attorney, I would not want to see him taken advantage of in his weakened condition."

The doctor nodded in agreement, "I agree, I'll see to it that he's not disturbed."

It was now time for Sean Kilgore to get to work. His next stop was going to be the Sheriff's Office to see what he could learn about the accident. He got the basic facts from the Sheriff and looked over Marlin's wrecked car. He found out who the witnesses were and how to contact them. No criminal charges had been filed as yet so it was now time for him to do what he did best… confuse the issues. He went to the Coroner's Office and spoke with the Coroner and pushed for a quick decision. He related to the Coroner that he had known Marlin for many years and how he and Mary Luzzetti were in the process of eloping. He pointed out the tragic circumstances and how badly Marlin was doing. As he did this he sized up the Coroner, studying him, before he made his next move.

"You know," he commented. "A Coroner's inquest is an open hearing... something the family would like to avoid... reporters... unwanted publicity... especially when you already have the answers you need. If I'm not mistaken, all an inquest would show is who, when, where, and how the girl died... a cause of death. You have all that information, right?"

"Yes, we do have that information," the Coroner replied. "But there is the matter of if the driver was drunk at the time of the accident, especially if his intoxication contributed to her death."

"True... but that falls into the jurisdiction of the District Attorney, right? Those are facts which he must prove. That issue could not be brought up in your inquest... only the matter of what physically caused her to die. You could not, nor would I expect you would want to go into that area... beyond your jurisdiction... especially since you have not examined my client or have any physical evidence to present. I think you can see that any speculation in that area on your part could be detrimental to my client as well as to you... it might open not only your office, but you as an individual to a civil law suit."

"What are you driving at?" the Coroner asked. "Are you implying..."

Sean cut him off mid-sentence, "Please don't get me wrong. I'm not implying anything other than I know how hard it can be sometimes when a Sheriff or D.A. puts pressure on another office to delve into matters outside their jurisdiction to the benefit of their department without considering the legal implications.

Besides; when you look at the entire matter it really is just a tragic accident."

He pointed out again that a quick decision for no inquest in the matter would be considered a great favor perhaps requiring additional work on his part. As he left he placed an unmarked envelope containing cash on the Coroner's desk and simply stated, "Marlin's family would not want you to go unrewarded for your extra work and service." The Coroner said nothing, just took the envelope and placed it in his coat pocket. He knew Sean Kilgore was right. It was out of his jurisdiction and doing the bidding of the D. A. or Sheriff wasn't going to be to his advantage in any way.

Next, it was time to find Sam Wiggins. Sam lived about fifteen miles out of town not far from where the accident took place in an old run down shack. He did just enough farming to get by and hired out as a farm hand. He was known as a drinker and a fighter. He was no stranger to the law and had occasionally been in some trouble. When he arrived at the house, Sean found him working on the old truck, pounding out the dent where he sideswiped Marlin. Sam had no feelings of regret or guilt over what he had done. In his mind, stealing the cash and pouring the liquor on Marlin was just his way of bending a bad situation to his advantage. Besides, why should he care what happens to some rich kid, he had his own problems to deal with. When he saw Sean drive up he became suspicious immediately.

As Sean got out of his car, Sam approached, "Who are you mister? What do you want?"

"My name is Sean Kilgore, I'm an attorney."

"An attorney! What the hell are you doin' here? You lost?" Sam questioned. He didn't like attorneys... or anything else remotely associated with the law.

"I'm here looking into the accident you had where the young girl died," Sean responded. As he said this he watched Sam carefully to see his reaction. When he mentioned the dead girl he saw a reaction in Sam's face... a reaction he had seen many times; the reaction of a man with something to hide.

"I done told the Sheriff all 'bout that... you can talk with him."

"Oh, I have spoken with the Sheriff," Sean continued as he walked over to where the truck was being worked on. "That's how I found you... you are part of the accident."

"What do you mean... that boy, he hit me, then went off the road... I didn't do nothin' but get 'em some help!"

"Maybe yes, and maybe no," Sean commented in a thoughtful way. "I talked with the boy then went by the accident scene and looked it over some, you know, just to get a feel for how it happened. By the way, you didn't find any money around the car did you? Seems my client had a substantial amount with him... it seems to be missing."

"I didn't see no money... all I done was get some help. What you drivin' at mister?"

Sean was careful about what he said. He knew that most people, especially guilty people, seem to think attorneys have some magical power to find or know things. Sean just planted some seeds to see what would happen.

"You know there may be a hearing in a couple of days and you'll be called to testify," he commented as he took a closer look and showing special interest at the damage on the truck. He made a motion as if sniffing an odor from the truck and while he didn't actually smell anything he thought he would take a shot at Wiggins anyway. "What is that smell... kind of smells like bourbon," he commented in an offhand way.

Wiggins was rattled and did what a rattled man does... he lied, "Might be... I was drinkin' some out here by the truck... I was shook up... you know, from the accident... might have spilled some."

"About that hearing... you will be available to testify won't you? I will have some very pointed questions to ask you on the stand."

Sam Wiggins stiffened up knowing that he had just been subtly threatened, "You're damn right I'll be there... I got nothin' to hide... you best be on your way!"

Sean smiled at him knowing full well he was scared and lying, "Very good, I'll see you at the hearing."

As soon as Sean pulled away in his car, Sam went into the house and packed a bag. He had the money he stole and was planning to be far away at the time of any hearing. Sean had done his job. As an attorney, it wasn't always a matter of facts in a case as much as a matter of confusing the issue in your client's favor.

*Chapter 5*

# Negociation Time

Marlin's family arrived in St. Augustine a day after Sean Kilgore and checked into the Ponce de Leon Hotel, the finest hotel in St. Augustine. Kilgore met with them and explained that he believed there would be no Coroner's Inquest but he had not met with the District Attorney yet. After the meeting they went to the hospital to see Marlin.

Marin was doing better by that time and was capable of answering questions but had not spoken to the Sheriff yet. There were a few mentions of the accident in the Charleston papers but the few details left a void and fueled gossip. Marlin was well enough that the family had him moved to the Ponce de Leon where he could be kept in seclusion.

George Reilly was playing his part as the concerned step father well, but made it a point to not interact with Marlin too much. Marlin was deeply depressed over Mary's death and George had been the primary person objecting to his seeing her. In his mind, if George had not objected so strenuously to their relationship they may not have been forced to run away and Mary would still be alive.

The next morning Sean Kilgore was scheduled to meet with the District Attorney. Prior to the meeting he sat down with Ruth and George to explain his strategy and what he planned to do. They sat down over coffee and he started his explanation but directed his comments primarily to Ruth.

"Ruth, I plan to push the D.A. to make a decision today... either charge Marlin with something or we plan to leave town. I will allow Marlin to provide a statement... a short statement, but the fact is there are few if any questions he could provide answers to."

George Reilly butted in, "Do you think that's wise, maybe..."

Ruth was not about to allow George to make any decision with regard to her son and she quickly cut him off, "Be quiet George, I have complete trust in Sean's abilities... I know he will do what's best for Marley."

George could see his plan to gain favor with his wife was not working but he kept pushing, "I should go to the D. A. with you, I'm sure I could help."

Kilgore looked at Ruth and she simply stated, "No, Sean will handle this matter." Then she looked at her husband and directed,

"You can make arrangements for us to leave to head back home as soon as Sean says we can go." With that Sean Kilgore left to meet with the D.A. and George Reilly went off to make the arrangements.

Sean Kilgore arrived at the St. John's County District Attorney's Office and was brought in. It was a somewhat old and dreary office. The walls were of a dark wood and there were the usual shelves of law books. It was cluttered and messy and Kilgore noted it. In his view it was like looking into the mind of his adversary. A man's office can be a reflection of the man. A neat, orderly office reflected an organized, efficient, prepared man. This was the office of an overworked, possibly lazy, elected official. The Sheriff was there along with the D.A. and neither one looked pleased. "Good morning gentlemen," Sean opened.

The D.A. stood up as did the Sheriff and extended his hand, "Good morning, I'm William White and I believe you know the Sheriff."

"Yes, the Sheriff and I have met," as Sean shook his hand. Then he sat down and got right to business. "Well Mister White, do you plan on charging my client with anything?"

"That all depends… the Coroner advised me that an inquest will not be necessary but we still have not been able to obtain a statement from your client."

The District Attorney was a middle aged man and there was nothing that stood out about him. He had the look of a man who ran for public office as a retreat from hustling up steady legal work to support himself. He had a tired, rumpled appearance and wore a pair of wire frame glasses down on his nose as he looked over the paperwork making an attempt to look studious. He looked over the young polished attorney in his office and made a critical error confusing his youth with lack of experience or knowledge.

Sean took some notes out of his briefcase, "My client is doing much better now and we would be fine with giving you a statement but just so you know, all he's going to be able to tell you with certainty is that he saw the bright lights which blinded him, was hit by the other car, heard Mary scream, and that was it."

"How much did he have to drink before that accident?" the Sheriff blurted out.

Sean expected that and didn't react, "I can tell you with certainty that Marlin had nothing to drink before or after that accident."

"Oh come on..." the Sheriff retorted before he was cut off by the D.A.

Sean went on, "Let me forward a few questions that I have for you. Did you find a bottle of liquor at the scene? No. Was there any test conducted to see if Martin had consumed any liquor? No. I checked on your deputy who was at the scene. He didn't even look for any liquor bottle at the scene. There wasn't one in Marlin's car. He didn't find one on the ground. Did he look in the other car? Again, no, he didn't."

The D. A. stated, "The deputy smelled a strong odor of liquor... so did the ambulance driver as well as the hospital staff."

"I'm sure they did," replied Sean. "However, after he was cleaned up and his clothing removed the odor was gone and I have a statement from the doctor saying that he was not responding as a person who was drunk. Very odd... suspicious, don't you think. This doctor is a man who has many years observing people who have been drunk or suffered head trauma... a very strong witness."

"Well, we have Sam Wiggins testimony... he was first on the scene," the D. A. countered.

"I have the second man's testimony... the man who went for help. He can't say for a fact he smelled any liquor at all," Sean replied calmly. "And as for Sam Wiggins... how reliable a witness is he. The information I have on him... well, let's just say his checkered past could place doubt on his credibility. My client had a great deal of money with him at the time of the accident and that money is now gone..."

"Are you saying Wiggins took the money?" the D. A. interjected.

"What I'm saying is that there is considerable doubt that my client was drunk. If he were as drunk as you think he was, how did he drive so far before he had the accident? What I'm saying is he may not have been responsible for the accident at all. Maybe it was Wiggins. Maybe he set up my client and stole the money as well."

"You have no proof of that," the Sheriff pointed out. "What proof do you have that there was any money?"

"Well, it's much more likely that my client did have money with him than not," countered Sean. "It would seem unlikely to run away to get married and not have any money with you... especially if you came from a family that has money."

"But you still have no proof," the Sheriff insisted again.

"Exactly... and other than the statements you have and what must be considered an unreliable witness in Sam Wiggins, you have no proof either. Certainly nothing you could go to court with and prove beyond a reasonable doubt... and don't forget that I will be able to provide character witnesses for my client... you have any for Sam Wiggins?"

Kilgore paused a moment to allow a response but when none was received he continued, "And let's not forget the accident scene... I went out there. There is nothing in the report that determines who was on the wrong side of the road... other than Wiggin's statement. It rained shortly after the incident took place. No physical evidence was left or noted to support who was on the wrong side of the road... evidence that could prove my client innocent. Need I say that I will not let that level of incompetence go unaddressed in court!"

The Sheriff took offense to that comment, "Listen here, we do the best we can down here..."

The D. A. cut him off at that point knowing that Kilgore had more than enough to show reasonable doubt and provide sufficient levels of incompetence to damage his career. As elected officials, neither he nor the Sheriff could afford to have a slick big city attorney make them the laughing stock of Saint John's County and Saint Augustine. Come election time there would be plenty of rivals who would be quick to bring it up again.

Sean Kilgore waited a moment for his logic to sink in then continued in an effort to soften the blow, "Let's look at this incident for what it is, a tragic accident... an accident where blame or responsibility cannot be definitively proved... just a young couple in love trying to elope with a horrible ending. Don't you think he's suffered enough? With as little as you have, don't think I won't play that card against you as well!"

D. A. White looked over at the Sheriff and shrugged his shoulders. The Sheriff just rolled his eyes and looked down at the floor. The D. A. then concluded, "Okay, this is what I need from you.

I need the Sheriff to take your client's statement which I expect will be as you stated. With that piece of information we can close the case and no charges will be filed. It will be determined to be an accidental death... there will be nothing to keep you in Saint Augustine. Now all I have to do is explain to her parents..."

"I can assure you that we will do all we can to help Mary's parents," Sean stated. "While it was an accident, Marlin was driving and his family is distraught over the death. I will be personally contacting the girl's family to do what we can to help them through this difficult time."

Sean Kilgore had been right; the D.A. wanted the easy way out. If it had been an easy case... a case with notoriety where he could make a name for himself, he might have forced the issue. The victim and driver were from out of town... there was no local connection or reason to risk his reputation against a sharp, well versed attorney like Sean Kilgore.

The D.A. and the Sheriff instinctively knew that Marlin's family would be making a payoff to avoid a civil suit. The matter was officially closed as a fatal traffic accident with no criminal charges filed and the family left Saint Augustine to head back home to Charleston.

*Chapter 6*

# George Reilly

Marlin had been home for a few weeks and had recovered physically but not emotionally. He had tried to visit Mary's parents and they refused to see him. He was still depressed and the situation between him and George was tense. He had spoken to his mother at length about the incident and she was understanding and sympathetic. Ruth was forgiving in nature, especially with regard to Marlin and Alice. She had believed she was doing the right thing for her children and herself when she married George Reilly but over the years it proved to be the wrong thing to do. While they were married, it was as if they lived alone in the same house… they had moved to separate bedrooms years ago.

Sean Kilgore had made contact with Mary's family and made a financial settlement. Her father was not sophisticated in these matters and would have been easily taken advantage of by an attorney as skilled as Kilgore but it was Marlin's family's wish, specifically Ruth, that they be dealt with fairly and with compassion. Her father believed that Marlin had been drunk no matter what anyone would say and he was responsible for her death. He believed he should have been prosecuted and the only reason he was free was because his family had money. While there was more to it than that, it was true that without money and a skilled attorney he might have been prosecuted and found guilty. In the end, a great deal of money settled the matter but the truth was that no amount could bring Mary back or heal the pain.

Very little was said in the newspapers because very little was ever brought to light. Marlin's family would make no comment and it seemed the press wasn't really interested in the opinion of Mary's parents other than to throw doubt and suspicion on a wealthy family. The Sheriff and District Attorney in Saint John's County covered their tracks well to avoid embarrassment, referring to the matter as just a tragic accident. Sam Wiggins had disappeared for the time being. Still, people gossiped about the incident and that made things very uncomfortable for Marlin and his family.

The tension between Marlin and his step father grew. There were heated arguments at times almost coming to blows. George continued to point out that Marlin would be in jail if it weren't for him… making sure to point out that if Marlin had listened and not become involved with Mary she might still be alive. He made sure he did not make these comments anywhere near Ruth. He continued this mental torture until one day Marlin had enough.

Marlin wasn't large for his age. He was tall, thin, of a lean, muscular build. He was not skilled in fighting but could hold his own with someone of his own size in a fair fight. George Reilly however was a large, heavy, bully of a man. He was well versed in drinking and fighting. He liked to intimidate people but especially Marlin believing he had something to hold over him. One day he had been drinking and his verbal abuse of Marlin went too far. Martin had come in the house and walked by the study where George sat drinking.

"Where have you been?" George demanded.

"Just out for a while," Marlin replied, not wanting to interact with George.

"I'm surprised you can still walk around and show your face in this town, considering the shame you brought on this family," he taunted.

Marlin turned to walk away but George continued, "How does it feel to be a murderer? How did you feel when you killed off that little whore?"

Something at that moment just snapped in Marlin. George was laughing as Marlin approached and punched him in the face. George took a step back, seemingly unfazed by the punch.

"I've just been waiting to see how long it would take for you to take a shot at me," he said as he grabbed Marlin by the front of his shirt and punched him hard, breaking his nose. He punched him again, knocking him unconscious as Alice stepped into view and screamed. On seeing Alice, George dropped Martin to the floor and stormed out of the house.

Calvin the butler came running when he heard the scream. "Calvin... help me!" Alice screamed as she went to Marlin's aid.

Calvin helped her get Marlin onto a couch and then went to get some water. He regained some of his senses as Alice and Calvin were cleaning him up.

"Lie still," ordered Alice as she cleaned his face.

"I'm alright... I don't know what happened Alice... I just... I don't know."

"I'm surprised you ain't tried to kill that son of a bitch before this!" Calvin commented in an uncharacteristic way. "Oh, I'm sorry Miss Alice..."

Alice and Marlin were surprised by Calvin's comment. Calvin wasn't particularly well educated but he was always very proper. He had been with the family before they were born. He was a trusted friend as well as an employee but always held his opinion to himself unless asked. While he was always polite to George, Marlin and Alice always suspected he didn't like him, but this was the first time he had verbalized it. His uncharacteristic comment caught them off guard and broke the somber mood. The three of them started to laugh.

"I'm okay Calvin... no need to fuss."

Calvin wasn't convinced, "Well, your nose ain't okay. I'll see if I can't fetch up some ice for that."

Marlin and Alice were now alone. "I'm going to have to leave Charleston," he started. "I can't stay here anymore."

"Where would you go? This is your home, you can't leave... what about mother?"

"I have no choice, I have to go… there's too much here that…" Marlin paused for a moment. "There's too much that reminds me of Mary… all that has happened. I know what people are saying… they might not be as cruel as George, but some are thinking the same thing. Besides, Calvin is right… if I stay here and George keeps pushing, I might just kill him. That would hurt mother and the family more than if I just go away for a while, okay?"

"Then you will come back?" Alice questioned.

"Sure, I'll come back, but it might be some time before I do. I'll leave a letter for mother and I'll write to you when I get settled someplace. It's about time I got out on my own anyway. I've got some money to get me by… I've just got to go."

"When will you go?"

"Now," he replied. "I don't want mother to see me this way… it will just cause more problems. I'll write to you and Sean… I'll include letters for mother but only you and Sean will know where I am and how to reach me… you've got to promise! I don't want her to worry and I don't want George to know where I am."

*Chapter 7*

# The Shamrock Isle

Marin packed up a few belongings and left the letter for his mother. He knew she would understand but he also knew that no matter how he worded things, she would worry. He had been giving the matter of leaving Charleston some thought since he got back from Saint Augustine. He headed down to the harbor... the *Shamrock Isle* was in port.

Captain Michael O'Shea was the captain of the *Shamrock Isle*, one of several ships owned by Marlin's family. Captain Mike, as he was known was a rough and tumble man of the sea and had been one of his father's closest friends. He was a large, bearded man who had been at sea most of his life and was considered one of the family. He was like a favorite, fun loving uncle to Marlin and Alice... a man they knew they could always turn to. The family shipping interests were large and Captain Mike was offered a powerful position in the company many years ago but he just couldn't stay on land, preferring to have a ship under his feet. If anyone could be trusted to help him slip away from Charleston it would be Captain Mike. He arrived at the ship and went aboard, proceeding directly to the Captain's quarters. He knocked on the door and heard the unmistakable voice answer.

"Aye... enter!"

Marlin opened the door and found the Captain seated at his desk looking over some charts and paperwork with his little dog, a Pembroke Welsh Corgi named Pee Vee, seated at his feet. He looked up and saw the boy, "Aye Marlin, 'tis you! Come in, come in!" Then he noticed Marlin's damaged face, "What the hell happened to you? You been fightin'?"

Marlin explained the situation and Captain Mike frowned, "Never liked that bastard... should pay 'em a visit... see how he likes tanglin' with Captain Mike!"

"No Captain... all I want to do is see if I can ship out with you on the *Shamrock Isle*... with all that's happened, I just need to leave for a while... but I can't have them know where I've gone!"

"Aye, I understand... but what of yer mother? She'll be worryin'"

Marlin went on to explain how Alice would take care of things, how he left her a letter, and how Sean Kilgore would look after things. Captain Mike finally agreed, "Well, a young man must leave the nest sometime an' what better way than ta go ta sea! It'll be a grand adventure for ya... now we'll have a look at that nose, it's surely broken!"

"It'll be okay," Martin stated.

"No, it won't be okay! If I don't fix it a bit you'll have an ugly nose pointin' sideways... look at some a me crew... plenty with ugly noses from bein' broke. It won't be like it was, but it'll be better than it is."

Then Captain Mike opened his desk drawer and took out a bottle and two glasses. He poured some Irish whiskey into each glass, "'ear you go... drink up!"

Marlin looked at the glass and hesitated. Captain Mike looked at him and pointed out, "The first thing ya gotta learn on a ship is ta follow orders! Especially if the Captain be the one givin' 'em, so drink up an' I'll be fixin' yer nose!"

Marlin choked a bit when he drank the whiskey and within a short time, Marlin felt a little light headed. Captain Mike poured him one more and ordered him to drink it down. Marlin drank it down as ordered and the Captain downed one more as well. "Well, now we're ready an' I can be doin' some doctorin'"

Captain Mike calmly took Marlin's nose and quickly pulled it back straight. The boy winced slightly and the Captain commented, "Now ya see why I gives ya some whisky... hurt like hell if I didn't." Then he took some medical tape and taped up the nose for some support. "Now, ya best be lying down in me bunk and be hidin' out 'til we shove off. Once we're out ta sea I'll introduce ya ta the crew. They all are good boys... good sailors. Get some sleep an' don't be getting' up an' bangin' that nose into nothin'! We'll be leaven' the tape on for a while… 'til the swellin' goes down… you'll have a right fine nose, broke just right… add some character to your face! Show that ya been scrappin'… ya can't trust a man who don't have a few scars on 'im."

He helped Marlin to the bunk as Pee Vee watched. The little brown and white dog hopped onto the bunk with Marlin, licked at his nose and then curled up at his feet. Captain Mike started laughing as his little dog settled in to watch over Marlin, "I'll be attendin' ta some business before we shove off. Looks like Pee Vee didn't think I done enough… had ta get his licks in! He'll be watchin' over ya 'til I come back."

*Chapter 8*

# One of The Crew

It was early the next morning when Marlin woke up. His nose throbbed as well as his entire head. It took him a moment to get his bearings before remembering where he was. When he realized he was in Captain Mike's cabin on the *Shamrock Isle* he started to get up but was dizzy so he waited a moment before attempting to rise again. He could hear shouting of commands and the sound of the ship's engines. There were sounds of chains scraping and the loud thuds of things being banged about. Pee Vee gave him a quick lick on his face before jumping off the bunk as the ship was getting underway.

Marlin was now standing... a bit unsteady, but standing, when Captain Mike entered the cabin. Pee Vee barked a quick greeting and bounced around at the captain's feet. "I see yer alive! Pee Vee seems ta think you'll live! Maybe I missed me callin' in life... perhaps I shoulda been a doctor... a man o' medicine. How ya feelin'?"

"My nose is throbbing on the outside of my head and the inside of my head... well, it feels like my nose!

"I can only be takin' credit for the inside head throbbin'... that bein' from some good Irish whiskey! The nose come with you already damaged. Yer head will be better in a few hours but yer nose will take a few days. Stay in the cabin 'til I comes for ya... when we're out ta sea."

It was about three hours later when Captain Mike came back to the cabin. Marlin was feeling a bit better by this time... at least the inside of his head was, and he was ready to get out of the cabin. When Captain Mike entered he made an announcement, "I met with the crew an' explained yer situation. Yer now part of me crew an' your sailor trainin' will begin. The boys are happy to have an extra hand on board an' they'll keep yer secret. Black Johnny is gonna show ya around so ya git yer bearin's."

When they stepped out on the deck the sea breeze was fresh and crisp. It immediately refreshed and invigorated Marlin. A short, balding black man in his forties approached the Captain. He was muscular and walked with a steady grace on the moving ship like he had been doing it all his life. "So this is your stowaway Captain!"

"That he is!" answered the Captain. "Marlin, this be Black Johnny. He'll be showin' you around, learnin' ya 'bout the ship. He's a good sailor... been all round the world so pay attention."

"Marlin?" Black Johnny questioned. "You're named after a fish?"

Marlin wasn't taken back with the question... he'd been asked it before, but Captain Mike offered up the explanation, "That's a fact! I was in the Caribbean with his father when he catches a blue marlin. He said it was the strongest, most beautiful creature he ever saw an' I had ta agree. He says to me, Captain Mike, if I ever have a son I believe I'll name him Marlin an' I tells him I think it's a splendid idea... but most of his family an' friends call him Marley."

Marlin followed Black Johnny and his lessons at sea began. As they approached the bow of the boat, the lesson began. "My full name is John Pierce," he began. "They call me Black Johnny because there's another Johnny on board and he ain't black... he's White Johnny. Just so you know, I don't take no offense to bein' called Black Johnny... it ain't no secret to me, I know I'm black."

Black Johnny smiled as he explained his name and Marlin almost laughed. "Out here," he continued, "Things is different than on land. Nobody cares what color ya are, we all just do our job an' we get along fine. Capt'n Mike is a good capt'n an' a fair man."

Marlin asked, "Do you know where we're heading? I never even asked Captain Mike."

"Africa," Black Johnny answered. "Our final destination will be Africa, but we'll be stoppin' a few other places in South America first."

They were at the bow of the ship and Black Johnny was beginning Marlin's training with a tour of the ship. "I'm goin' to be takin' you everywhere on this ship so you can find your way around... an' you'll have to be learnin' how we talk on a ship. The front is the bow, the back is the stern... when you face the bow, starboard is on the right, an' port be on the left."

As they moved about the interior of the ship, Black Johnny noticed that Marlin seemed to lose a bit of his color. "Boy, you look a little green 'round the gills... let's get up topside." As they reached the upper deck Black Johnny instructed Marlin, "Get to the rail an' puke over the side. No sense in tryin' to hold it back. It may be a little bit o' seasickness or it might be from Capt'n Mike's doctorin'... just look at the horizon and breath deep. Nothin' better than sea air."

After throwing up and a few minutes of sea air, Marlin was game to continue. Black Johnny however took pity on him. "We'll be stayin' topside for awhile... there's plenty more things we can learn without bein' below decks for a while."

They sat on the deck and began instruction on how to tie the variety of knots a sailor needs to know. Marlin threw himself into his studies and focused his mind on learning all he could. It kept his mind from wandering and thinking of all that had happened. Over the first week Black Johnny kept him busy and would assign him to work with the other men on the ship so he could learn something of what each man did. Marlin took to the life at sea. He enjoyed the banter of the men and at first he didn't understand their course language and humor. He soon realized that it was just their nature and that they were good, honest men.

Captain Mike called him to his cabin one day after about two weeks at sea. "I see yer nose is lookin' better. I see I was right... it will give ya a fine dash of character... gives ya a look of a man who's been around... seen a bit of the world."

Marlin smiled at the Captain's comments. The swelling had gone down but it was still sore and he wasn't all that sure how good it looked but there was nothing to be done about it now. Captain Mike motioned for him to sit down. "You been doin' well with your learnin' ta be a sailor. Black Johnny been teachin' you well. All these men know who you are... I mean, they know yer family owns this ship, the company, and all. Most of the older men knew yer old man... he would come down to the ship for a visit an' always he'd bring some good Irish whiskey for the boys."

Marlin waited as the Captain paused for a moment. He clearly was going to say more. "The men know of yer troubles an' why you left Charleston from the newspapers. Many of these men came to sea because they had problems to leave behind. Yer old man believed in givein' a man a second chance. Know that men will tell you of their past on their own terms an' you can do the same... know that no man aboard will ask you what happened. You've made a good impression 'cause you're learnin' to be a sailor an' not flauntin' yer heritage."

"Black Johnny tells me we're bound for Africa... is that true?"

"Aye, we're bound for Africa but we will make stops along the way in South America. We drop off some cargo and pick up more, then in Africa we unload what we have and load for the return to Charleston. You run along an' be getting' back to work... weather looks like it's about to change an' the crew will be makin' ready for a storm."

Marlin went off to find Black Johnny to see what he could do to help. He found him with the other men busily checking lines and tie downs. He jumped right in and started helping. He could feel the change in the air as the wind picked up and the sea changed color. The change took place quickly as the deep blue water changed to dark grey. The clouds started to form and then it rained. Not the gentle spring rain but a flood of water from the sky as if they were under a waterfall mixed with the crack of thunder and lightning. Black Johnny grabbed Marlin and yelled to him over the sound of the storm, "Remember... one hand for you an' one hand for the boat... always hold onto something... you go overboard an' yer gone!"

As it got later in the day the swells rose and the ship groaned as it climbed up one swell and came down on the opposite side. The water crashed over the decks and no one went outside unless there was business to attend to. Marlin was at one level excited and on another level scared. It seemed like the ocean was about to swallow up the *Shamrock Isle* at any moment. None of the other men seemed the least bit apprehensive about the storm and just went about their business as best they could. Marlin was in the galley with a few of the men along with Pee Vee when the Spaniard, a thin swarthy dark haired sailor, came looking for Marlin. "Marley, make your way topside to the wheel house. Captain Mike is gonna show ya how to sail this ship."

A few of the other sailors heard the order and started laughing and giving Marlin a bad time. "Boy, pay attention up there... don't be sinkin' the ol' *Shamrock Isle*. Hey, Spaniard... you remember where we keep those life jackets?" Another sailor dropped to his knees as Marlin was leaving folding his hands as if praying, "Lord, watch over us as Marley takes control of the *Shamrock Isle*... if this be our end, please let it be quick and painless!"

Pee Vee went over to his little bed in the galley... one of several sleeping spots he had on board. He would normally have gone off to the wheel house with Marlin because it was his favorite spot on the boat. His short little legs and low slung body made him stable under most sea conditions but he was not allowed to roam around the decks during a storm. He was a pampered member of the crew that no one wanted to lose. As he curled up and stuck his nose down under his paws one of the sailors commented to Marlin, "See that! Be careful... Pee Vee don't want to be goin' swimmin'!"

Marlin made his way to the wheel house, getting soaked in the process. When he entered he found Captain Mike and William, the first mate talking as they steered into the raging storm. "Aye, it's Marley... William you can go below and git yerself some coffee. Marley and me will be in command!"

William left the wheel house and Captain Mike began the lesson. "Every man aboard this ship knows how to steer her... some better than others and only a few on a regular basis, but none the less, it's ta be part of yer education. The sea is a livin' thing an' ya got ta pay attention... see how I be keepin' her bow into the wind an' into the swell."

Marlin was paying attention but from up in the wheel house the storm looked even bigger than when you were on the deck. The peaks of the waves looked like they were ready to go over the top of the ship then they would drop down and the ship would drop to the bottom of the swell and you would be looking up... the ship slowly climbing the swell, to repeat the process. "We aren't going to sink, are we?"

Captain Mike laughed, "No boy, we ain't gonna sink... least I hope not! It's good you ask that question... always believe that the sea will sink ya and ya will never take her for granted. The sea is like a woman… ya can never take her for granted! As soon as you do, you'll be in for a surprise! Maybe a surprise ya won't like! Never think your boat is too big to be sunk because any boat can be sunk. The *Shamrock Isle* has been through bigger storms than this. This is a small storm, but you always have to be careful."

"It looks pretty big to me!" Marlin commented as a large wave broke over the bow.

"That's only because this be yer first storm… nothin' to compare it to! Come here… take the wheel. See the compass heading? Stay on the heading… adjust the ship after each swell."

Marlin took the wheel nervously and could feel the massive ship respond. They went through a large swell and he could feel the ship start to be forced away from the course. "Steer back into it… back on the course… keep the ship straight into the swell… if the ship were to go sideways, we'd be rolled over," ordered Captain Mike. "There ye be. Never go faster than the sea will allow, just enough to stay in control, ta stay on course, an' not beat up yer ship… ya can only take what the sea will give ya… speed an' schedule be damned… take to bein' safe."

Marlin stayed on course for four hours and before long the fear of steering the great ship left him but not the caution. Captain Mike reminded him of how much responsibility there was in the safe operation of the ship… not just the cargo and money involved, but the lives of his shipmates. It was a physical task as well as a mental one. It took effort … physical strength against the sea, to make the ship go where you wanted. He began to understand what Captain Mike meant… the sea was so powerful it just seemed you had to go with it and be part of it. It did feel alive. To Marlin it felt like he, the ship, the crew were all being held in the palm of a giant hand and being allowed to live... but in an instant, without warning the hand could close and they could all be taken. As big as the *Shamrock Isle* was, Marlin felt very small and humbled in the vastness of the sea.

The first mate came back to the wheel house. "Aye William, what do you think of this young sailor... has he what it takes?" asked Captain Mike.

"He seems to be takin' to it Captain. Perhaps we can make a sailor of him yet! I'll be relievin' you so you can be havin' some dinner. Looks to be calmin' a bit."

"What you say Marley... steerin' this ship give ya an appetite? Let's go below and have some chow. William, I'll be sendin' a second man to assist ya. Remember Marley... we always have two sailors in the wheel house. One to steer and one to check charts, navigate... and as a second set of eyes!"

When Captain Mike and Marlin entered the galley there were several men seated and they all stood up. Several yelled, "Well done!" while the others clapped their hands. Marlin looked at Captain Mike not knowing what to think. "That be for you boy! Yer first time at the helm... steerin' into the storm. They know yer one a them now, like yer ol' man... once a man feels a ship under his feet, it's in his blood, no goin' back. You can be in the middle of a desert but in yer heart, you'll always be a sailor!"

Marlin soon learned that Captain Mike was right. The sea was a living thing filled with life that stayed hidden from view most of the time. When the sea was calm sometimes the creatures within it would let themselves be seen. The whales, porpoise and sharks would show themselves and give a glimpse of their life in the sea. Seabirds would be seen swirling and diving when the sea boiled with schools of fish trying to avoid the bigger fish trying to eat them from below. The more time he spent at sea, the more he felt the rhythms of the sea... the connection of the ship and the sailor in those rhythms. He came to understand that once the ship sailed out into the ocean, the ship, the sailor and the sea became one... but the ship and sailor weren't needed by the sea. The sturdy ship and the wise sailor would be allowed to stay and to live... the unsafe ship and the foolish sailor would perish.

*Chapter 9*

# Black Johnny and The Spaniard

One day while Marlin, Black Johnny, and the Spaniard were working topside Marlin asked Black Johnny, "How long have you been at sea... a sailor?" Black Johnny continued working and answered, "Oh, let's see... about twenty years or so... ain't that right Spaniard? Twenty years or so?"

"Si... about right... we start with Captain Mike about same time."

Marlin was careful in his question. He made it a point not to ask why he went to sea in case there was a personal issue like in his own case. Black Johnny sensed that and appreciated how the question was asked. "I went to sea to see the world," he laughed. "Actually, I went to sea to make money an' 'cause it seemed like a great adventure... an' 'cause your ol' man gave me a chance."

Marlin perked up at that comment. He was young when his father died and he only knew him in the light of how a child sees his father, a caring adult male, a trusted parent, he knew little of him as a man... how he lived his life. "What do you mean?" he asked.

"Times were hard back then... I guess there are hard times now as well, but I was lookin' for a job an' went down to the docks. There wasn't much work for white men let alone a black man an' it wasn't seen fit for me to be down there. I got into it with a couple a white boys an' your father broke it up. He talks with me awhile an' says let's go up an' see my friend Capt'n Mike. So he takes me to this office and there sits Capt'n Mike. Your father says to Capt'n Mike... he says, this here is my cousin Johnny an' he wants a job as a sailor."

At that point, the Spaniard starts laughing almost uncontrollably at the vision of Black Johnny being introduced to Captain Mike as Robert Colby's cousin. He had heard the story many times and it always made him laugh.

Black Johnny continued, "Well, Ol' Capt'n Mike, he just looks me up and down a bit an' looks back at your father an' without even cracking a smile... he looks at him and asks... Black Irish is he? An' your father says... yeah, on my mother's side o' the family. Then they both start to laughin' an' I don't know what to think."

The vision of this encounter now had them all laughing. After a moment, Black Johnny continued, "So we talked for a while an'

I learned that most of the crew were Irish... there wasn't a lotta love for the Irish back then either... anyway, I went to sea an' been a sailor ever since."

"But what about family? You have any family?" Marlin asked.

"Oh yeah, I got family... I got a wife an' kids back in Charleston."

"It must be hard to be away from them."

"Remember Marlin, it ain't how much time you spend with someone, it's what you do with that time. You were young when your ol' man died, but the time you had with him made an impression... he couldn't help dyin' young an' I can't help bein' a sailor, it's just who I am. It's provided a good steady income for my family... more than I could make on land. One day I'll be sendin' my son to college... besides they seem to appreciate when I come home that much more... now the Spaniard, he's lead a real sailor's life... tell'im Spaniard."

The Spaniard was a quiet, dignified man, who had a charming quality about him. He didn't say much, but when he spoke, the other men listened. Marlin suspected there was more to him than he let on, but didn't pry. He seemed to be modest, even shy, but anyone could see he knew his way around a ship.

Black Johnny continued, "Yeah, the Spaniard, he was a merchant sailor during the last war... had two ships torpedoed right out from under him... in the North Sea no less, an' he lived through it."

It seemed the mere mention of the sinkings brought back bad memories. You could see it in the face of the Spaniard; his eyes took on a faraway look. Marlin moved away from the topic, "What's your given name... your mother didn't name you Spaniard, did she?"

The question lightened the mood for the moment, "No… my given name is Ricardo Espinosa, and I was born in Madrid. I went to sea when I was about ten."

"Ten!" Marlin exclaimed. "How did you do that?"

He spoke in a calm, quiet voice, "In Spain, my family was poor. I was fortunate to be placed as an apprentice… instead of going to school, my school was the sea, I was sent to be a sailor. Later I came to the States and became a merchant sailor. I did survive two sinkings… I was very lucky… there were only a few of us who lived. I also knew your father and he was a sailor… sometime you ask Captain Mike about it."

The Spaniard gave no other details but Black Johnny filled in more, "The Spaniard ain't married, but there's a lot you can learn from him kid… he's got a girl in every port! If you want to get laid just hang around with him, the ladies love him!"

The Spaniard just smiled a wicked little smile and commented, "I do okay."

*Chapter 10*

# Cartagena

The *Shamrock Isle* docked in Cartagena and the stevedores on the dock started unloading cargo. The crew was ready to hit the town except for a couple of sailors who stayed with the ship to oversee the unloading, seeming a bit apprehensive about even being seen. Marlin found Captain Mike getting Pee Vee ready to go into town. The little dog had been brushed and the captain had placed a small white sailor's hat on his head that was secured with a rubber band between his erect ears. The little dog didn't seem to mind the hat and seemed anxious to go on an adventure. Captain Mike was all dressed up in his going ashore clothes. There was something a bit comical in the large, gruff looking bearded ship captain with his little Corgi wearing a little white sailor's hat but Marlin thought better of laughing. He just looked at the pair and commented, "I see Pee Vee's ready to go to town."

"That he is!" replied Captain Mike. "Here's a bit o' advice. If ya want ta meet women, all ya need is a little dog. They'll be flockin' 'round ya in no time… it's even better if the little dog wears a sailor's hat!"

Marlin could no longer hold back the laughter as Pee Vee stood there wearing his hat and wagging his stubby little tail. Captain Mike laughed as he put a leash on Pee Vee. "He don't like the leash much, but if I don't put it on 'im he'll get loose an' he'll be off humpin' every little bitch in town. Before long there'll be little Corgi dogs everywhere… ya know, he's like the rest o' us… been out ta sea for a while!"

"Captain Mike, how did you come to name him Pee Vee?"

"Pee Vee stands for 'Perpetual Voyager' which is what he is… but ya can't call a dog that! He's a fine little sailor for a Welshman!"

Captain Mike was heading for Maria's Cantina, a bar and whore house just a few blocks off the docks. The Spaniard, Black Johnny, and Marlin were dutifully following Captain Mike and Pee Vee along the dirty, bustling docks. Captain Mike would occasionally yell a greeting or a curse at people he knew along the docks. People waived, shouted greetings back or pointed at the Captain and Pee Vee walking down the street.

"I'm surprised the crew left behind didn't get angry," Marlin commented. "I would expect they would want to go to town… besides, I'm the newest crew member so I should've stayed behind."

"Well, normally you'd be right 'bout that," replied Black Johnny. "You see, the last time those boys were here there was a little trouble. There was a fight an' a guy got himself stabbed. I'm pretty sure they didn't do it, but if you're the stranger in town you're likely to take the blame. We sailed before they ended up in jail so we don't know how it all ended… they may have got the one who done it. Not knowing' an' all… well, this isn't a town where you want to end up in jail! We'll ask around a bit and see if the coast is clear. Until then they'll be lying' low."

Maria's Cantina was the gaudiest building on the block. It stood apart as it was painted bright yellow with red trim. There was no attempt to disguise the fact that any and all of the vices were available just inside. Captain Mike burst through the door like he had been away at sea for years and shouted in a booming voice, "Where's Maria?" The place got quiet for an instant until everyone realized it was Captain Mike and then they all started to cheer.

From the back of the room came running a short chubby woman in her late forties wearing a red dress that she was almost bursting out of. She was trying to balance as she was running in her high heels and screaming, "Capitan Mikey! Capitan Mikey!" Her long bleach blond hair was in sharp contrast to her dark skin. When she got to the Captain she flung herself into his arms and started kissing him wildly.

"Yes Maria, it's me! Back from the sea. Did ya miss me? Have ya been faithful ta me while I been away all this time?" he asked as he gave a wink to Marlin.

Maria looked shocked, "How could you ask such a thing? You know I love only you!"

With the grand entrance over, Maria led the group to a table towards the rear and drinks soon appeared. Marlin had never seen such a place in his life. Music was playing; people were drinking, gambling, and dancing. Smoke filled the air, it was noisy, and there were girls everywhere. Captain Mike sat in a chair at the head of the table like a king holding court and Maria sat herself in his lap. Twenty years earlier, Maria was a beauty who decided the best way use her talents was to become a whore. She did so willingly and twenty years later she was the richest woman in Cartagena.

"Maria, this young fella is Marley. This bein' his first voyage an' all, have a few of your loveliest girls come over an' take a look at 'im... give 'im some special treatment... I'll be takin' care of the tab."

Maria looked over at Marlin and thought if she were only a few years younger she would give him some special treatment herself. "I have lots of nice girls... they come over. A girl for Spaniard and Johnny, too?"

"Not me," replied Black Johnny. "Thanks the same, it's a temptin' offer, but I guess I'm just old fashioned an' married."

"Well... let's have some drinks!" Captain Mike ordered. "Whiskey for the boys... beer in a saucer for Pee Vee... no whiskey for Pee Vee... he gets mean when he drinks whiskey!"

All this conversation was taking place and Marlin was just looking around, awestruck by the atmosphere. Men were openly carrying guns and knives, there was a minor fight going on in a corner of the building that was in the process of being broken up. Tobacco smoke filled the air and everyone was drinking and in high spirits. The whole place had a feeling about it that at any moment the earth would open up and it would be sucked straight into hell... it was exciting and he liked it. Within a few minutes he had consumed his drink and was working on another. A pretty young Hispanic girl wearing a very seductive low cut dress was now seated close to him. She was whispering in his ear a language he couldn't understand but he didn't care. Whatever she was saying sounded sexy and inviting.

Pee Vee was doing his part... every woman in the place at one time or another came over to the table to see the little Corgi wearing the sailor hat. They would fuss over him as he drank his beer in the saucer at Captain Mike's feet.

Captain Mike raised his glass in a toast, gave Marlin and the young girl a look and a wink while everyone raised their glasses, "To the making of memories an' the loss of innocence!" Everyone was laughing, including Marlin, although in his mildly intoxicated state he really didn't know exactly what was going on.

The next thing he knew Marlin was dancing with the girl and she was pressing herself close to him. Marlin had a warm uninhibited feeling as she took him by the hand and led him upstairs to her room. There was an air of excitement mixed with a little hint of danger as he entered. She was a beautiful young woman and sensed that Marlin was not experienced in matters of sex. She also felt an air of excitement in the taking of his virginity and was enjoying the moment. He wasn't like the horny sailors she was used to and she was intent on making his experience a memorable one.

Marlin had just enough alcohol to stay in the twilight area between passed out and unable to perform. His first sexual experience was with a young woman who had perfected her craft and enjoyed the experience as much as he did. He lay with her in bed for a time, partly to recover his senses a bit and partly to enjoy the moment a while longer. Finally he got up, got dressed, and found his way back to where his group had been only to find Black Johnny the only one seated at the table.

"Where's Captain Mike and the Spaniard?" he asked.

"The Spaniard left with a woman about an hour ago and Captain Mike is with Maria getting reacquainted. I have had just enough to drink so now you an' me are goin' back to the ship while I can still walk an' not have to be carried. Don't worry 'bout 'em... they always find their way home."

*Chapter 11*

# Following His Father

All the while he was on the ship Marlin would hear stories of his father. It brought back memories of his time with his father that he hadn't thought about in a long time, due mostly to the conflict he faced with his step-father and the death of Mary. Being away at sea gave him time to reflect and men like Captain Mike, Black Johnny, Spaniard, and the others helped him to see the world and problems in a different light. They were all men who had lived... men who had seen the world, overcome problems, and seemed the better for what they had endured. While he still thought about Mary and what had happened, in the light of what some of the other men had experienced it was beginning to seem like what had happened was just a misfortune of life. He still felt the pain of it all and a sense of responsibility but as he was learning from his shipmates, there was no going back, there was no way to fix what had happened, there was just trying to keep living.

He was also able to think back on the times he spent with his father… the special times when they spent time together and what he had learned. He remembered going to the docks to see the ships and how his father spoke with the men who worked for him. He didn't treat them rough handed but spoke with them respectfully. He was confident. He was in charge and everyone knew it. There was no need to be heavy handed. He remembered his father saying, "But there for the grace of God go I." A phrase Marlin didn't understand at the time but fully understood now. If it weren't for his smarts, ambition and a high degree of luck he might have remained a sailor on a ship like all the others.

He thought about the times his father took him fishing or when he bought him a small twenty gauge shotgun and taught him to shoot… against his mother's wishes. He took him to hunt pheasant and rabbits out in the country then had the cook prepare them for dinner. It seemed the time at sea gave him more insight into the man and what he took from their short time together.

Marlin stayed at sea on the *Emerald Isle* for two years. He wrote to his mother and sister through Sean Kilgore and his step father had no idea of where he had gone. In that time Marlin grew and flourished. He saw the world and became a skilled sailor. Of all the places the *Emerald Isle* visited the most interesting to Marlin was Africa. One day Marlin had a talk with Captain Mike about leaving the ship and staying in Africa for a while.

"Captain Mike… can I have a few moments?" he asked.

"Of course Marley… what's on yer mind?"

"Captain, I was thinking I might like to stay in Africa for a bit. It seems like such a wild, untamed place, like no place on earth I've ever seen… maybe get a job and see the land."

"Are ya tired a bein' a sailor?"

"No Captain, it's not like that… it's just that there seems to be something about this place… I don't know how to explain it."

"Well, maybe I do," replied Captain Mike. "Africa was a special place to your father too. He was one of the first to open this area to shipping… at least in the modern era; there has been trade here for centuries. He took some time here as a young man… mind you now, it was years ago… it's now 1932 so some things have changed but Africa is an ancient place an' some things don't ever change. Since your father died young, learning 'bout him… who he was… what he did, means you have ta learn 'bout him from others. Ya don't have the opportunity ta ask him questions or sit an' get 'is wisdom in his old age. Funny thing how life works… when yer a youngster yer parents take care of ya an' when ya get ta be 'bout fourteen or fifteen ya get out on yer own. If yer parents stay alive ya get ta go back an' learn from 'em after ya make some mistakes… maybe find out 'bout their life before they became yer parent… learn from 'em as an adult."

Marlin listened to Captain Mike as he became more reflective. "Your parents had a life before ya came along… an' they have one after ya go out on yer own… most children get ta talk with their parents as an adult an' learn 'bout 'em… in your case that ain't possible. Ya heard 'bout his life at sea from the men here that knew 'im… ya have the memories of 'im from when ya were young… you've heard stories 'bout 'im from yer mother… maybe you should learn 'bout his time here in Africa."

"Where should I start?" asked Marlin.

"Leave that to me," replied Captain Mike. "The boys will miss ya on the ship, but I know you'll be back… the sea is part of ya now… it will always be a part of ya. I'll introduce ya to a man yer father knew here in Africa… that will be a good start."

*Chapter 12*

# Africa

C aptain Mike and Marlin traveled on an old train for almost two days. As the train rolled along at a slow pace the African countryside spread out before them. It was just as Marlin had imagined it would be… rolling hills, vast plains and more animals than you could count. The train made a few scheduled stops and several unscheduled to let animals clear the tracks. When they reached their destination they hired a driver who drove them far into the bush country. They didn't arrive until it was almost sunset on the third day. The road was nothing more than wide animal trails leading into the heart of the country and it was a long, hot, dusty ride. The further inland they got, and the further away from the sea, the more uncomfortable Captain Mike got. It seemed there were animals everywhere and being in a car rather than a large train didn't appeal to Captain Mike. He had no desire to observe the animals up close. They finally arrived at a large estate where it seemed there was lots of activity. It was a grand looking place, a large main house and several out buildings. There were fenced in areas, with some crops and it had the look of a farm or ranch.

Captain Mike looked the place over, "Well, this be the place... an oasis in the middle of this God forsaken land. What do ya think of it?"

"I don't know," replied Marlin. "Is it a ranch? Or a farm?"

"Not completely. They do raise some crops here but just enough for them since they are way out here. This place is a huntin' lodge. Rich folks from Europe and America come here ta hunt wild game... an' they pay plenty for the privilege ta do so. The owner is a fella name of Daniel Crowley... Bwana Dan... he's the great white hunter 'round here. He hunts everything out here; rhinos, elephants, hippos, leopards, but especially lions... he's the number one lion hunter... that's why all those rich folks come here. He and your father were good friends. Your father was a little older than you when he came here. He an' Crowley hunted together."

"Are we going on a safari?" asked Marlin.

"I ain't... but maybe you are. I got no love of all this land... all them animals just waitin' ta eat me... I'll be happy ta get back ta the *Shamrock Isle*...but if ya want to see Africa, then Crowley's your man. He's always lookin' for help out here... especially white men.

He's got plenty of tribesmen out here, but he's always lookin' for someone who his guests will be comfortable with. Some of these tribesmen are scary buggers."

The driver stopped in front of the great house and a few natives came running to take their bags. Captain Mike looked uncomfortable in his surroundings and apprehensive. He looked over at one of the native workers and asked, "Where's Bwana Dan?"

The native smiled when he replied, trying to be helpful and polite, "Bwana Dan he go. Come back sometime."

Captain Mike led the way into the house and commented, "These guys always make me nervous... they might be damn cannibals for all I know... they look like those damn cannibals I run into in the South Pacific... those bastards will cook ya up an' eat ya! I guess if we're gonna wait we might as well have a drink."

He walked behind a bar that was situated in the great room. There was a variety of mounted heads and horns on the walls as well as several zebra hides on the floor serving as rugs. Photos of hunters posed with their kills were scattered about on every wall. Several large well stuffed chairs and ash trays were scattered about and it was clear that this was the room where the guest hunters drank, smoked, and shared the stories of their hunts. There was a stone fireplace and prominently placed over it was the head of a very large African lion. A formal dining room was adjacent to the great room and a kitchen attached to that. Upstairs were several guest rooms and an office but Captain Mike pointed out that the guests and workers have their own cabins not too far from the main house.

Captain Mike made himself right at home and seemed to be a bit more at ease now that there were no natives around. He poured them each a drink and they sat down to wait for the return of Bwana Dan. Marlin had by this time become a better, more seasoned drinker having been to more than a few ports of call and bars. He sat down and took in his surroundings before asking Captain Mike, "So Captain, you mentioned cannibals in the South Pacific... what happened?"

Captain Mike took a sip of his drink and a sour look came over his face recalling a bad memory. "We was in the South Pacific at the time... I was a youngster back then on a sailin' ship... near a place called Papua New Guinea. We was told that there be cannibals on some o' the islands but we didn't believe in such things... thought they be tellin' us that ta keep us from goin' ashore an' havin' some fun. Some a those islands, the women don't wear hardly no clothes an' are very friendly to sailors. We figured they was tellin' us 'bout cannibals ta keep us away from their women. So a few a the crew take a long boat an' head in... me goin' along as well. So we get ta the beach an' there be no one around... very quiet... spooky. Then we see this little dark man almost naked an' he's got a bone through his nose. I guess him an' his friends was watching us out on the ship. He starts yellin' somethin' and comes at us waivin' a spear. As soon as he starts yellin' a couple more come out a the brush an' they look just like him. Well, it scared the shit outta us and we start headin' back to the boat... but them little devils start ta chasin' us an throwin' them spears. One of the boys had a gun with him an' he turned around an' shot one a the buggers. A spear caught him on the leg an' cut him pretty good but he was able to make it back ta the ship. I think he killed the cannibal bugger but we didn't go back an' find out... these here native boys remind me a them cannibals only they be taller!"

Marlin sat mesmerized by the story. While Captain Mike was prone to exaggerate the facts of a story at times, he could tell by the expression on his face that this story was true. Captain Mike got up and helped himself to another glass of whiskey and began to tell Marlin about Daniel Crowley.

"Ol' Dan," he started. "He was born out here in Africa... loves the place. Parents were missionaries... come way out here from England ta bring Jesus ta the savages. Back then they had the London Missionary Service, sendin' out missionaries. Dan's father at one time had been a hard drinker 'til he got the faith. His momma was a real bible thumper... straight laced... no drinkin' or cussin'. They wanted ta stay in England but the old man didn't have the political connections in the church so they was sent ta Africa... they thought it was gonna be temporary... a proof a their faith, but they got stuck out here. As you can see, they didn't have much success in civilizin' the savages... fact is, after a while they couldn't civilize Dan... when he got ta be 'bout twelve he started rebelin' like most boys do. There be no other whites around here back then so his friends are all natives. His parents want him to become a preacher like his father an' they think he be bringin' the word to the savages but he's just goin' about learnin' their ways... how ta track and how ta hunt. This is a hard land... brutal an' unforgivin'. By the time Dan is sixteen his mother has died out here of ta fever an' his father is a broken man... he loses the faith after his wife dies an' starts back ta drinkin'. Dan hires out as a big game hunter until the ol' man dies... eventually sets up his own business."

"How did my father fit into the story?" asked Marlin.

"Yer ol' man was always one ta be lookin' for some adventure. So when he's out here he wants ta go huntin' an' meets up with Dan. They hit it off an' do some huntin'... but he was more than a huntin' client. He an' your ol' man were kindred spirits... they loved ta hunt and they loved the untamed wildness of this place... he stayed on here for a time, huntin' with Dan. As his business grew he had less time ta come back... then of course he met your mother, married, an' started a family."

"Seems almost like his life as a sailor and hunter was interrupted by responsibility," Marlin commented.

"No... it weren't like that. Your ol' man loved yer mom... you an' yer sister more than anything else. Sailin' an' huntin' are what a young man, like your father, does while he's travelin' 'round lookin' over the world... maybe findin' his place. What your ol' man did was build a shippin' business... build a family... build a life... he did what he wanted ta do. He found the right woman ta settle down with."

"What about you Captain... you ever going to settle down? Find the right woman?"

"Me!" the Captain exclaimed. "Look me over Marley... I'm an ol' barnacle! I find the right woman in every port I visit... but I'll not settle down. Especially not in a God forsaken place like Africa! No, I'll be stayin' on me ship, sailin' the high seas... where all these hairy beasts won't be tryin' ta eat me... that be ta reason I didn't bring Pee Vee along... some lion woulda eat him for sure! Don't get me wrong... there been a few women tried ta Shanghai me an' get me ta marry 'em but I'd have none of it."

Then Captain Mike gave Marlin a sly smile and said, "If ya decide ta stay out here in Africa workin' for Daniel... after ya get ta know him an' he trusts ya... get 'em ta tell ya the zebra story... but don't ask 'em when there be other people around... ya might even wait 'til he has a few drinks in 'im!"

It was getting close to sunset when they heard the sound of a vehicle approaching. The truck stopped in front of the house and there was much excitement amongst the natives. In the back of the truck was a dead Kudu and the natives began scurrying as Daniel Crowley and another man stepped out. Crowley gave a few directions to the natives and the two men entered the house. He stopped short when he saw that Captain Mike was inside waiting for him.

"Well, if it isn't Captain Mike!" he stated in surprise. "What a surprise to see you... especially so far from the sea and in the middle of Africa. To what do I owe the pleasure of your visit?"

*Chapter 13*

# Bwana Dan

Daniel Crowley was not what Marlin had expected. He expected a tall, lean, muscular man wearing a pith helmet and carrying a large rifle. What he got was a man of about sixty years old, five foot eight, somewhat over weight, wearing a dirty khaki shirt and trousers, a dirty cowboy hat, cowboy boots and carrying a Colt forty five on his hip. His hair was mostly grey and shaggy and it appeared he hadn't shaved in a few days. He wasn't the vision of the great white hunter he expected. Marlin would later learn that Daniel Crowley had a fascination with the American West...

especially the western frontier and cowboys. His manner was formal in his speech but friendly and it was clear that he was glad to see Captain Mike.

"Daniel, I come all the way out here ta bring ya some much needed help," he began. "This young fella here is Marlin Colby… Robert's boy! He shipped out with me on the *Emerald Isle* over two years ago an' now he's thinkin' he'd like to see a bit o' Africa… even though I told him it's foolish."

"Robert's boy! You don't say! Well then, let me take a good look at you… yes, you do favor your father. I lost a good friend when he passed… he was a wonderful man. Welcome to Africa!" and he extended his hand in a warm handshake. "We'll have a drink… Captain, I hope you helped yourself in my absence."

"That I did… both me and Marley."

"Good… good," Crowley replied. "This is wonderful… Robert's boy here in Africa! Your father would be very happy about this." He went about pouring some drinks as he talked and then the second man walked in.

"Ah, Russell, come here, have a drink. This is Captain Mike O'Shea of the *Shamrock Isle* and this young man is Marlin Colby, the son of my dear departed friend Robert… gentlemen, this is Russell Durham, an American from Pittsburg, he's been hunting here the last few weeks."

Russell took his drink and explained that he had been making sure his prize kill was being properly cared for; at least the horns. The choice parts of the animal would be served up for dinner and the rest given to the natives for their dinner. Crowley encouraged Russell to relate the story of his hunt which he was more than anxious to do. Bwana Dan knew the one thing hunters liked to do almost as much as hunt was to talk about the hunt... share the story with other hunters or anyone else who could listen. It was part of the hunting experience that he was selling.

Marlin listened to the story intently and watched Daniel Crawley. He had not led the life planned for him by his parents. He was formal in his speech, an indication of his missionary upbringing, soft spoken and didn't swear. He was however a man who liked his whiskey and pipe but seemed to see himself as an American cowboy... six shooter and all. Russell gave an exciting account of how Bwana Dan and he stalked the animal for hours until he was in a place to take his shot.

Bwana Dan interjected, "You see Marlin, out here, my job as the guide is to get Russell in the best place to make his shot... it's his job to make the shot. Ah, but Russell is a fine shot and we got the job done!" It was unwritten, but it was also Bwana Dan's job to build up the hunter's ego, sometimes even when it wasn't warranted. Bwana Dan had perfected this role... the hunter could be horrible and Dan would make him feel good about himself and good about paying his outrageously high hunting fees.

Over dinner Captain Mike proposed that Marlin stay on and work for Dan. Captain Mike gave him a fine reference about his work on the ship and as expected, Bwana Dan was more than happy to have another white man working with him. Captain Mike pointed out that Marlin was strong and a quick learner... just what Dan needed. It was all true, since he left home at nineteen years old over two years had passed. The skinny boy that had shipped out was now twenty two, over six feet tall, and well-muscled. He had seen a bit of the world from a ship and was now eager to learn about Africa and what his father saw there.

"Marlin," Bwana Dan asked. "Have you ever fired a gun or done any hunting?"

"When I was young my father took me hunting for rabbits, ducks, quail, and sometimes pheasant... but that was a long time ago."

"That's fine... a good starting point. Tomorrow we'll fire some rifles and begin your training. In the afternoon you can come with Russell and me when we do some scouting. We're going to look for an elephant for him. Captain Mike, would you like to come along?"

"Thank ya but no!" replied the Captain. "I'll be leavin' in the mornin' after I see Marlin shoot the gun. Got ta get back to me ship. I expect that findin' somethin' as big as an elephant should be no problem... but I don't want somethin' big as an elephant findin' me!"

## Chapter 14

# Target Practice

Early the next morning the group sat down to breakfast. While they were far out in the African savanna, it appeared that Daniel Crowley was leading a fairly comfortable life. As the cook started to serve, Bwana Dan started to lay out the plan for the day.

"After a fine breakfast we'll go out and do some shooting. Out here a man's life depends on how well he shoots... often a matter of whether you get to eat or be eaten," he stated in a calm but factual tone. "I think we'll start Marlin off with the Mannilicher .256 and then have him shoot the Rigby .416. Russell, I would like you to get in a few rounds of practice with the H and H (Holland and Holland). That nitro express round takes a little getting used to and we'll be very close to that big bull... only two shots you know. I know you've fired it before but I can't have you missing your trophy!"

Russell perked up at the mention of the Holland and Holland. "That sounds fine Dan. I'll take all the practice I can. A gun that big requires practice, besides I want him to be the trophy... I don't want to be his!"

"After the practice shooting," Bwana Dan continued. "We'll head out to scout for that big bull. We'll find one with those big tusks that you want. I know a couple of places we might find them where there's food and water close by. They won't be moving around much right now... not much pressure on them with plenty of food and water. There's plenty of food roaming about to keep the lions away and there have been no other hunters out this way."

Captain Mike was relatively silent through the morning breakfast but after breakfast while Bwana Dan and Russell were getting the guns ready, he pulled Marlin aside. He was beginning to feel a sense of fatherly responsibility and envisioned Marlin being eaten by a lion or crushed by an elephant. "Marley, are ya sure 'bout all this? Are ya sure ya want ta stay out here in the middle a no where? I don't want ta be the one ta have ta explain ta yer mother how ya met yer end out here!"

Marlin smiled with that self-confident look that every twenty two year old has had... the look all young men have at an age when they don't believe they can be killed. "I'll be okay Captain. I'll stay. I'd like to see what it's all about. See why my father was so attached to this place."

The group proceeded to an area that had been set up as a firing range. It was used primarily for when a new hunter arrived and Bwana Dan would have them test fire their weapons. He used the test fire as an excuse to see how they handled their weapons and to see if they could actually hit a target. It would at least give him an idea of their ability to hit a non- moving target… the matter of whether they could stand and shoot a large attacking animal then became more of a matter of character. Often the natives who would be acting as bearers on safari would come to watch the shooting. While they wouldn't say so because they would be out of place, they had a vested interest in how well the hunters shot. Their lives on safari might be in jeopardy if the hunters didn't shoot well and sometimes if the hunter got his prize there might be some tip money in it for them.

After Bwana Dan explained the safety features of each rifle, how to load, shooting position, sighting, trigger squeeze, etc. it was time for a demonstration. He took the .256 Mannilicher and explained, "This rifle fires a 158 grain bullet at around 2450 feet per second… an excellent rifle for our thinner skinned deer type grazing animals. As the size of the animal goes up, so does the size of the gun."

He then took the rifle and shouldered it, taking careful aim at a target set out at approximately one hundred yards away. He took three shots in fairly rapid succession and then sent one of the natives running down range to recover the target and set up one for Marlin. When the runner returned he presented Bwana Bill with the target. There were three holes in a triangle shape about of about a one inch spread. He took the target and looked pleased as he studied it, then showed it to Marlin.

"There you go… that's what we want. Just don't fire as fast as I did… take your time with each shot… focus on the front sight and squeeze the trigger as you exhale… never pull or jerk the trigger."

It all sounded familiar to Marlin. It was the same instructions his father gave him years ago when he was teaching him to shoot… but the gun was not as big or loud. He went ahead and loaded as Bwana Dan gave him instructions. The native boys put up a new target and ran for cover fearing this new hunter would surely miss and hit them. Marlin shouldered the gun and took careful aim. He exhaled all the while focusing on the front sight of the rifle and squeezing the trigger. Suddenly the rifle fired and kicked back. Marlin recovered and chambered another round and repeated the shot twice more. When he was done, he opened the action of the rifle and gave the native boys the signal that it was all clear so they could run down range to retrieve the target without fear. They ran back with the target in hand and big grins on their faces.

Bwana Dan looked at the target and a big grin came over his face as well, "Look here Marlin… three holes… not as close a group as mine but three holes just the same. Well done for the first time with this rifle. Now we move up to the bigger rifles so you are familiar with them… then you practice each day until you can place three shots within a one inch circle. Now we will fire the .416 Rigby… my preferred gun for lions… a bigger 400 grain bullet. After that we fire the Holland and Holland .577 nitro express… the elephant gun… Russell will get in a few shots of practice before he stares down an elephant!"

Marlin fired the Rigby and while he was disappointed that the pattern spread was at about five inches, Bwana Dan was impressed.

"These big guns take some getting used to... that's very good. We work to get accuracy here. While that group will certainly kill most animals, the ones it won't are the ones that will kill you before they give up the ghost! Shot placement and accuracy are the most important thing out here because we move in close... a quick, accurate, fatal wound, that's what we want."

Bwana Dan asked one of the gun bearers for the Holland and Holland and sent some of the boys down range to move the target closer to about thirty yards. Then he began his instruction as he pulled two rounds of ammunition from his pocket, "We'll have Russell fire first. We move the targets in close because this is how close we'll be to that big bull elephant when Russell fires. It's hard not to hit an elephant, but if you don't hit him in the head and kill him, he'll be on top of you in an instant and he'll kill you."

Marlin watched closely as Russell loaded the rifle and Bwana Dan explained what he was doing. The cartridges were almost four inches long and looked like they were about one half inch diameter... they looked like they were the size of shotgun shells but were rifle cartridges. Russell was skilled and self-assured as he handled the gun. After he loaded his two rounds he placed two more rounds in his hand held between his fingers so if he had to, he could quickly open the weapon and reload. Bwana Dan told him that he would time his shot when he told him to fire. This would give him the time it would take him to shoulder and fire the big rifle and hit the target. Dan gave the command and Russell quickly shouldered, aimed, and fired. The rifle shot sounded like an explosion and Russell lost his footing when the gun kicked causing him to fall to the ground, dropping the extra rounds in the process. Russell was clearly embarrassed by the incident and as he got up commented, "That was a disaster! My foot slipped on a small rock... not good, not good at all. Did I at least hit the target?"

While the incident looked comical, Marlin was too shocked to laugh and noticed that none of the natives or gun bearers even cracked a smile. Each knew what it would mean to not make a shot on an angry elephant at that range. Bwana Dan had a grim look on his face and simply looked at the target and stated, "Well, you hit the bloody target... but you would have never made the second shot if you needed it! We'll do it again... but this time settle your feet in first and make sure you're stable. You might as well remember to settle in first because if you miss, you won't be able to move quick enough to escape anyway."

The atmosphere was tense as Russell practiced several more times with the rifle. He was an excellent shot and never missed his mark. Marlin was beginning to comprehend what was at stake and how the hunt would be accomplished. Bwana Dan would get Russell into position within forty yards or closer to an angry bull elephant and Russell would have seconds to shoot and make the kill... having only two shots available to him. He could have two more but only if he were extremely lucky and extremely quick... not a likely scenario. While the question occurred to him as to why anyone would willing place themselves in such a position he didn't ask. Before long it was his turn to fire the Holland and Holland.

"Okay Marlin," Dan coached. "Don't shoot fast, just brace yourself for the kick... lean into it and keep it tight to your shoulder. Fire the first shot, then brace up again and fire the second."

Marlin did as he was instructed and squeezed the trigger. The gun knocked him back but he kept his footing. He could now understand how Russell could end up on the ground. He braced himself again, aimed, and fired. He opened the action to show the gun was safe before the native boys retrieved the target. There were two holes in the target but they were not close together.

Bwana Dan looked at the target and pointed out, "The shot in the center was your first shot... the second shot you anticipated and jerked the trigger. It's hard not to anticipate the punch you'll get from the Holland and Holland... takes practice. That's enough for now. We'll head back to the house, get something to eat and head out to scout for the elephants. Captain Mike... sure you don't want to come along?"

"No, not me!" replied Captain Mike. "I'll be headin' back to the ol' *Shamrock Isle*. Marley has decided ta stay for a while an' be workin' for ya. If ya be getting' him killed an' eaten by one a these wild beasts, you'll be the one writin' home ta his momma!"

While the rifle practice had been going on, Marlin had noticed a tall Maasai dressed in the traditional red Maasai robe standing under a tree watching. He was tall, lean and held a long spear in his hand. He had a dignified, serious look about him and didn't approach the group of shooters or the other natives, just watched from a distance, almost as if he were studying them.

As they were leaving, he noticed the tall Maasai was gone. "Bwana Dan, who was the tall native watching us from over there?" Marlin asked as he pointed over to the tree.

"That would be Sironka... a Maasai warrior. He was probably getting a look at you and sizing you up since you'll be starting your hunting training with him in a few days."

# Chapter 15

# Elephant Hunt

C aptain Mike headed back to the ship. He was anxious to get back to the sea and away from the African interior. Bwana Dan, Marlin, and Russell set out to locate the elephant herd and plan the hunt. This would be Marlin's first excursion into the African plains and he was excited. They would travel by truck and then move out on foot, spending the afternoon hours looking for the herd.

As they were preparing to leave Bwana Dan called Marlin over and handed him a rifle. "You carry this gun," he said as he handed it to Marlin. "You never go out into the bush unarmed. The Mannilicher won't be knocking any elephants down but you shot it well and you need a weapon of some type."

The African elephant is the largest living land animal. A male can stand thirteen feet at the shoulder and weigh over 13,000 pounds. Both male and females have tusks that can be from five to eight feet long and weigh up to one hundred pounds. The shot placement to reach vital organs is between a third and half way up from the chest firing from the side of the animal. It's not recommended to take the frontal head shot, but many of the hunters want to face that challenge... including Russell.

They got into the truck and drove for some time. There was a dirt road for part of the trip and then they were just out on the plains. The going was slow and Bwana Dan was careful not to damage the truck. There were animals everywhere and Dan went about pointing them out as he drove. Russell wasn't the least bit interested in the other animals, his mind was focused on elephants. Not just in finding them, but in the task of standing in front of one of the giants and shooting it before it trampled him to death. He was quiet during the ride playing out the scenarios in his mind trying to visualize what would take place and building up his courage to make the hunt.

The time had now come to strike out on foot. They left the relative safety of the truck and headed towards a location near the river where Bwana Dan believed they might find the elephant herd. There was a completely different feeling from being in the truck to being out on the savanna. Marlin was at high alert, mindful of everything around him... expecting a lion to jump out and attack him at any moment. Russell was moving along, now in the mode of a hunter, comfortable in his environment. Bwana Dan seemed relaxed as if he were just out for a stroll but was more aware of his surroundings then the other two. They came up over a rise and could now look across a small valley towards the river. Dan took out a pair of field glasses and looked over the area. Then he called Russell over to him and handed him the field glasses, "Take a look over there... to the left of that bend... there's a pool of water there."

Russell looked through the glasses and exclaimed, "Elephants! Just look at them!" Then he handed the glasses to Marlin so he could take a look.

"We need to get closer to get a good look," Bwana Dan commented. "We'll have to circle to a point about a mile from here to see if we can spot a big bull with large tusks... stay down wind and see what we can see. They have plenty of food here and won't be moving soon... they should still be here or close by tomorrow... but if there aren't any big bulls then we'll have to look elsewhere. We have time to move in and get a better look then get back to the truck before sunset."

They hiked to a position about a mile and a half away and downwind from the herd. They were now close enough to hear the elephants. They were playing in the water, spraying water and mud over their huge bodies. Off in the distance about a quarter mile from the group was a large male moving towards the water. Bwana Dan handed the glasses to Russell and stated, "Take a look at him. What do you think?"

Russell took the glasses and when he looked through at the elephant a chill ran down his spine at the thought of confronting such an animal. The elephant was huge and had formidable white ivory tusks. "He's magnificent! Huge... just look at the size of those tusks!"

Dan asked, "So you think he'll do?"

"He'll do quite nicely," Russell replied.

Marlin looked through the glasses at the elephant. They were several hundred yards away and the beast looked huge from there... how would it look standing in front of it at about thirty yards. It occurred to Marlin at that time that maybe Captain Mike was right... what type of person would actively seek out the largest animal on land, intentionally sneak up on it... try to get as close as possible, then stand in front of it just daring it to kill you before you kill it. Yet Russell seemed elated and overjoyed at the prospect.

His thought process was interrupted when Bwana Dan stated, "Okay... let's get out of here before the wind changes or we do anything to spook them. We'll come back and start here early tomorrow and try to get Russell into shooting range."

It was dark before they arrived back at the hunting lodge. After dinner they all went to bed early because they had to be up well before dawn. Bwana Dan's plan was to arrive early in the morning when the elephants would be feeding. There was still plenty of food in the area so they wouldn't move until they ran out. They would still be close to the water but would not move to the river until they were well fed and the heat of the day would require a refreshing swim. After coffee and breakfast they headed back to where they had last seen the elephants. This time Dan brought the truck to a closer position and as the first rays of the sun lighted the savanna they began the trek to find the elephants. When they found them they were feeding as Dan predicted and they were on the near side of the river, not the opposite side. There was little wind at this early hour and the majority of the night predators were now finished with their nocturnal feasting.

It took hours to track and carefully move into a position where Russell could get a shot at the elephant. They were close now... within about sixty yards, but still not close enough. It was now the moment of truth. Bwana Dan was going to move Russell to a location where the large bull would be aware of his presence. The only way to get the frontal head shot and to confront the animal was to get him to look at Russell as a threat. The elephant would naturally move towards the threat and attempt to scare off the intruder. He would charge out of the brush, trumpet loudly and flare out his ears, which would cause most animals, including lions to flee. It's called a mock charge intended to scare the off the intruder. If it were a real charge, the elephant's ears would be pinned back and it would be a direct charge with no stopping. Today the elephant would challenge a man, the logical animal that would do the illogical, and the man had to be ready for anything.

Dan turned to Marlin, "You stay here. We're going to circle around and let the bull know we're here. He'll be surprised and angry and should come out and give Russell a shot. Don't stand up, just stay here where you can see what's going on. All the elephants will get spooked but they won't run right away, they'll try to bluff and scare us away. After he makes his shot, they'll run but should move towards the river. If they come this way, tuck yourself over between that tree and rock and just stay down."

Russell and Dan moved off a few yards and Dan had him double check his weapon one last time, partly to make sure he was loaded and partly to re-assure Russell that he was ready to go.

As they moved into position Russell could feel his heart pounding in his chest. There was so much adrenaline in his system now he was shaking. He was determined to stand and make his shot. They were now in a clearing and could see the large bull elephant in the brush, he had stopped feeding and his trunk was high in the air... he had detected the intruders but had not seen them. Bwana Dan now had Russell slowly stand up and he stood just behind him and to his right. Both men had their guns at the ready, but this was Russell's hunt, he would have to take the first two shots... Dan would only shoot as a last resort.

The huge elephant now saw them and came charging through the brush. He swung his massive head back and forth, trumpeting, and stomping his feet... then he moved back into the brush. Bwana Dan put his hand on Russell's shoulder, "Steady now. He'll move in and out again... just wait. Get your gun up... he'll charge out again and stop for a split second to size us up. That's when you take your shot."

The elephant again charged through the brush and this time into the clearing coming closer this time. He was now within about thirty yards, his ears flared out and his massive head lowered. Russell had planted his feet and had the gun raised to his shoulder. In that split second he squeezed the trigger and there was the explosion of the gun firing. The shot was true and the elephant dropped to his knees momentarily stunned as Russell quickly took aim and fired the second shot. The large bullets had struck their target, crashing into the skull and destroying the animal's brain. The elephant let out one last anguished groan and fell to its side. As Bwana Dan had predicted, the other elephants fled towards the river. Russell stood there for a moment taking it all in but no longer shaking. He had never been so scared and so happy at the same time. The next thing he knew, Bwana Dan was shaking his hand and congratulating him, "Well done, excellent shot! We'll get some photos!"

Bwana Dan had a camera in his pack and had Russell pose with his prize for some photos. After he had a few with just Russell in the photo, he had Marlin take a few of himself and Russell with the elephant. The photos were all part of Dan's marketing of the hunt. He would make sure Russell was provided with a copy so when he got back home he would talk up the great hunt he had with Bwana Dan in Africa.

This was the first large animal Marlin ever saw being shot and killed. As a boy he had shot pheasant and rabbits with his father and hadn't really given a great deal of thought to the process. At the time he was so happy to be with his father and because his father was excited over his kill, he was excited as well. This was the first time he was a detached observer to a hunt and it was a mixture of fascination, repulsion and excitement. On one hand there was this massive, beautiful beast living free in the wild and harming no one. Then there was the killing of the beast and the slaughter, the dis-memberment and the trophy. Finally there was the facing of your fear... the facing of death and the excitement of surviving the chal-lenge. Marlin then remembered something his father said to him when he was just a boy... something he had not thought of in years.

His father told him it must always be ethical to kill an animal and that any life should not be wasted. If you killed a rabbit, it must be for food, not just to kill it for the sake of killing something.

Within about forty five minutes a group of native tribesmen arrived on the scene and began butchering the elephant. Marlin watched as they cut away the massive tusks and several of the men started walking away with them. "Where are they going," he asked Dan.

"They're taking the tusks back to our truck," he explained. "They'll be here for awhile cutting up the elephant... lots of food for a long time."

A part of Marlin was repulsed at the sight of the natives butchering the elephant and a part of him was fascinated. The men worked feverishly cutting the large beast to pieces. There was almost a rhythmic cadence to the operation as they melodically disassembled the animal.

"Nothing will be wasted," Dan commented as Marlin continued to watch. "They'll make quick work of it and take what they want... before the scavengers come around. Out here, death is a magnate. All the animals need to eat and most don't want to work hard at it... an already dead animal means you don't have to hunt for it or risk injury during the hunt. Just find the dead animal and dinner is served! Let's head back."

*Chapter 16*

# The Maasai

It was the next day when Marlin's formal training was to begin. He had breakfast with Bwana Dan and used the occasion to ask about his teacher. "So who is Sironka?" he asked.

"Sironka is a Maasai... one of the largest tribes out here. He's trustworthy enough, probably more than most." Bwana Dan had good relations with the natives but still considered them inferior and not always reliable.

"I noticed he is always dressed in red and he is very tall. What are the Maasai like? What are their beliefs?" Marlin asked.

"The Maasai... they're special, they'll never be tamed. They're nomadic herders, but don't let that fool you, they're a warrior people. Back in the 1890's they had a Civil War amongst themselves. There were a couple of brothers named Senteu and Lenana and each wanted to be the Laibon, which is the community spiritual leader, a very important position to the Maasai. It was known as the Morijo Civil War and it was about that time they came into contact with the British. The Maasai fought the British and got their asses kicked. On top of that the British exposed them to smallpox and the epidemic killed off many more. Eventually the Brits were able to use the brother's rivalry and took up sides with Lenana. After Senteu was defeated, Lenana became Laibon and it wasn't long after that that the Brits moved them out of the Rift Valley so it could be settled. Europeans by that time had claimed Africa as theirs and started to colonize."

Bwana Dan was somewhat of an enigma. His parents were ill suited to bring the Christian faith to Africa and life was extremely hard for them with little support from the church. While Dan identified with the white Europeans there was a part of him that objected to them being there. He was in the strange position of being the rare white person born in Africa at that time. It was his home and while he had been indoctrinated by his parents to believe the natives were a lesser person than himself, which was the widely held colonial view, he also knew that in many ways they were capable and to be admired. Having never lived in England and not knowing exactly what civilized living was he had no real comparison. He held a certain level of contempt for those that came after him and their way of life... their pretense of civilization in the middle of the most uncivilized place on earth.

"Where did they move them?"

"To someplace they didn't want at the time." Dan continued, "Sort of the same thing that was done to the American Indians in your country. They've been moved several times since. Some of the Maasais even became mercenaries, working for the British against other tribes who resisted colonialism... kind of an interesting twist. Many of their customs and beliefs don't sit well with the whites."

"Like what?" asked Marlin.

"They believe in a God, a Deity, sky and rain... they call it Enkai, but they don't believe in an afterlife... with a few exceptions. The soul of a Laibon or a rich man may turn into a snake in the hereafter and they don't bury their dead, the bodies are put out for hyenas. They place them to the west of the village with the head facing to the east... towards the sunrise. The Laibon or rich man might be buried in a shallow grave covered with some stones. They live primarily on cow's blood and milk... maybe with a few vegetables now and again, but mostly on blood and milk... rarely meat if a cow dies but not wild animals."

Marlin looked at him in disbelief, "How can that be? Blood and milk? It sounds disgusting!"

"It is," replied Dan. "They puncture a vein on the cow and take some blood. Then they mix it with milk... sometimes the milk is fermented or soured... doesn't matter to them and they drink it. They will take some mud or dung and seal up the wound on the cow so it will heal up. They are herdsmen... cows are a measure of a man's worth... the more cattle the richer the man."

"I don't think I could drink that... even if I were starving," Marlin commented.

"If I was starving and I had a cow, the last thing I would be thinking about would be drinking blood! I'd be thinking *steak! Lots of steak!*" Dan commented with a laugh before he went on. "One of the more interesting customs is that when a woman marries a man she is actually marrying all the men of his age set. They are the men who went through the rites of passage with her husband... sort of like marrying all the guys in your high school graduating class, but on a smaller scale. Here's the interesting part, each one of those guys can sleep with her anytime he wants and the husband is required to give up his bed! I understand she can refuse the guest but I don't know how often that happens. On top of that, he can have more than one wife. I guess he could go to his friends hut and give his wife a try if he was of a mind to."

"No wonder the missionaries had a hard time out here!" declared Marlin. "That's a lot for Christianity to overcome. I can see why the whites would find them uncivilized, but I don't know; it seems to work for them. At least it has for centuries. What do you think?"

"I saw my parents die out here trying to bring their God to these people. They believed they were doing what was right but in the end, Africa drained the life from them. They really didn't change much. Who's to say one God is any better than the next. Who's to say if there is or isn't any after life. It's a savage existence out here... kill or be killed, today you're a hunter, tomorrow you're a meal. As far as being civilized... I've seen plenty of goings on with the aristocrats and settlers up in the Rift Valley. They act virtuous and Godly... proper and sophisticated, but there's plenty of sleeping around going on with them as well. At least the Maasis aren't pretending; it's out in the open. Maybe I've been out here too long Marley… it seems the older I get, the less any of it matters to me either way."

Bwana Dan sat there for a long moment thinking over the situation. He had been in Africa his entire life, for the most part not thinking over his situation or questioning the world around him. Marlin unintentionally brought a new view of Africa. His simple questions caused Dan to look at things he hadn't really thought about in years. "It's really rather silly when you think about it," he began. "White men like Livingston and others came here to explore Africa claiming to have 'discovered' whatever they found. They might have been the first white men to see something, but they didn't 'discover' shit. How can you discover something that's been there all along? It didn't exist until you came along? Nobody who lived here knew it was there? It doesn't exist until a white man says it exists? It doesn't have a name until you give it one? All bloody stupid when you think about it."

Before they went outside to meet Sironka Marlin asked, "What does the term 'Bwana' mean? Why do they use that term to address us?"

"It's a term of respect," he replied. "It's Swahili and translates to master or boss. Out here you are always Bwana Marley to them… don't ever forget that and don't let them forget it either. My parents always said it was the white man's role in Africa to save the savages from themselves… they have a soul that needs to be saved, provided they accept God but they're still savages… some just tamer than others."

When they went outside after breakfast they found Sironka standing under a tree waiting for them. Dan did the introductions,

"Sironka, this is Bwana Marley. Marley, this is Sironka, a Maasai warrior and a great lion hunter... he will be your teacher. He will begin your training with tracking and identifying animals and learning their ways. You will end each day at the rifle range perfecting your shooting skills."

Marlin extended his hand and Sironka shook hands with him as was the tradition of the whites but said nothing. Bwana Dan continued, "He is the best tracker out here and is smarter than all these other darkies combined... plus he speaks very good English. If you pay attention he will show you all you need to know to hunt out here... you'll have far more knowledge in a short time than the tourist hunters who come out here."

Marlin was curious about Sironka but for the time being just followed his lead. He was tall and his complexion was very dark. He wore the bright red attire of the Maasai tribe and a necklace made of lion's claws. He had a confident, regal appearance to him and carried only a long spear and a knife. His dark eyes had a serious, deep, complicated look but they were not menacing, but more inquisitive. The first words he spoke were, "Come... follow me."

Sironka led Marlin away from the house and straight into the surrounding savanna. Marlin followed him and they walked in silence for about thirty minutes before Sironka stopped and directed Marlin's attention to the ground. He knelt down and pointed out a hoof print in the dirt. He simply told Marlin what type of animal made the track and the direction it was going. He did this several times and then as they walked he pointed out the specific animals that made the tracks. Then he reversed the roles and directed Marlin to locate the tracks of specific animals followed by pointing out the specific animal on the plains. Sironka went about his teaching duties in a very methodical way. He made corrections but offered no encouragement and the two young men studied each other as the teaching process continued.

Marlin judged him to be a few years older than himself and felt that in some sense he was testing him. He moved through the land smoothly, confidently, as if he were part of it while Marlin moved through it as an innocent, not fully knowing and understanding all the dangers surrounding him. He found him to be fascinating and found himself wanting to prove himself to the Maasai warrior.

Sironka watched Marlin carefully. He was measuring him to see if he was smart enough to learn and survive. Did he have the potential to learn enough to lead men on a hunt? The culture dictated that only the white hunters would lead the guests on the hunts, the black man was delegated to assist even though they were far more inclined to be the better hunters having had to survive on their skills to live. Sironka held no animosity with that arrangement. Bwana Dan treated him well and paid him handsomely for his services. He was not interested in killing the animals, only leading the hunters to the animals. While the motivation for hunting as the white men did puzzled him to some extent, his motivation was to stay alive during the process. Marlin's training and success would be critical to that process.

It was about noon when they stopped tracking and identifying and Marlin followed Sironka to the top of a hill. They stopped in front of a tree and Sironka directed Marlin, "Look into tree... all around it."

"What am I looking for?" Marlin asked.

"Anything hiding in tree... big thing like leopard... small thing like snake. Danger is not always on ground... sometimes above you." Then he tapped the tree with his spear while still looking into it. "Some animal will not move unless you wake them. You see animal?"

"No," Marlin answered. "I see no animals... nothing moving."

"Good, we sit and watch."

With that, they sat under the tree and from that vantage point Marlin listened as Sironka pointed out various animals on the savanna and told their stories. His narrative almost sounded like a children's story of how each animal lived, where it traveled, what it ate, where it would drink or sleep, and most important, what would kill and eat it. As a small herd of zebra came into view Sironka pointed them out and stated, "Watch... lion will catch one."

Marlin could see the zebra but there were no lions in sight. "What lions? I don't see any."

Sironka pointed to a spot where there was some high brush, "Four lions. Hiding from zebra... waiting."

Marlin looked at the spot and sure enough, after a few moments he could make out the lions. They blended into the grass almost perfectly, completely hidden. As he watched, one of the lionesses slowly moved away from the others to a position away from the others and moved closer to the herd.

Sironka pointed out, "They will take the zebra towards the end... he is weak, hurt."

Sure enough, Marlin could now make out a slight limp in the gait of the zebra and it did seem as if the lioness that moved away from the others had her attention focused on that zebra. It seemed remarkable to him that Sironka could so quickly spot the lions and identify the zebra they would target out of all the others. As he watched, the other three lionesses cautiously moved closer to the herd.

Sironka watched for a moment longer before stating, "Soon they take zebra."

A few of the zebra began to act nervous, either sensing or smelling the lions. As they started to move a bit more quickly the lions made their move. The three showed themselves and began to chase the herd, cutting out the weak zebra. Marlin had lost sight of the forth lion but then in an instant, it charged from the flank of the zebra jumping on its hindquarters and knocking it off its feet. As it fell, the other three pounced and one of them grabbed the zebra's throat in its powerful jaws and clamped down. The other zebra fled in a panic and as the captured zebra was still weakly kicking its legs, the lions started to tear it apart, pulling out the internal organs.

As the lionesses started to devour the zebra a large male lion appeared and made his way towards the kill. The females protested, their bloodied faces snarling, but yielded to the male. He ate for a time, occasionally chasing off a brave female who would get too close and as he became full, allowed the females to begin feeding. He slowly wandered off as the females continued to feast only stopping now and then to chase off the other animals drawn to the fresh meat.

Marlin was fascinated by the savagery of the attack. He had seen sharks feeding on a dead whale while at sea but this was different, he had not witnessed the sharks killing the whale, they were eating as scavengers. The lions hunted down the zebra, snarling and growling as they tore it apart, covering themselves with blood in the process. They sat there watching for about two hours and the temperature was now hot. Sironka rose and simply stated, "We go back now."

Marlin stood up and took his canteen of water, removed the cap and offered it to Sironka, "Here, have a drink." Sironka looked at him for a moment like he didn't understand and in fact he didn't. In general, white men looked at the natives as almost a lesser being. The offer of a drink from a white man's canteen was unheard of. Marlin pushed it towards him again and insisted, "Take a drink... it's a long walk back."

Hesitantly, Sironka took a drink of the water and handed the canteen back to Marlin. Marlin then took a drink and recapped the canteen. Marlin had thought nothing of this act and while he didn't realize it, he had just cemented his relationship with his teacher. In that simple act, he had shown him a level of understanding and respect not normally extended. On the walk back, Sironka had Marlin walk next to him, not behind him and pointed out how to walk through the savanna. He pointed out things that only a hunter would be looking for... and what the other hunters, the animal hunters would be looking for as well.

These lessons went on for weeks and as the two young men moved about the savanna their friendship grew. Slowly each grew to trust the other and shared the story of their lives. The other native men who worked at the hunting lodge seemed to view Marlin as different from the other whites... possibly from his relationship with Sironka or possibly by the way he carried himself and treated them. While he didn't forget what Bill had told him he understood that just because the native's lifestyle was different from his own, it didn't mean they weren't smart or perfectly adapted to life in Africa. Marlin had no designs on Africa like other whites. He had no desire to own or possess it, only to visit, learn and understand it. His only desire was to be out on the savanna studying the animals and to become competent enough to move about on his own. Often he would travel about with Sironka for hours both men never saying a word, just moving through the wild land.

Over this time his ability with a rifle grew as well and he became an expert shot... on a target. His ability had still to be proved on a live target in a hunting situation.

*Chapter 17*

# The Idiot Hunter

"Sironka tells me you are an expert tracker and can sneak up on any animal out there. Is that true?" asked Bwana Dan.

"I've learned a lot from Sironka but I don't know if I could be considered an expert," Marlin replied modestly.

"Well, today we'll have a bit of a test run. I'm going to be the tourist hunter and you're going to guide me on a hunt for an Impala. Your job is to get the idiot hunter into a position to shoot the animal and I will play the role of idiot hunter... after all these years out here you'll find me to be quite skilled at playing the idiot."

Marlin smiled at the comment and had an idea this test would be coming. Sironka had hinted that Bwana Dan might be taking him hunting and had prepped him for the test. Dan went off to get his rifle and hunting gear and Marlin went off to do the same. A short while later they met in the yard in front of the lodge. Several of the natives were curious and were watching from a short distance away. They had seen this test before and were anxious for Bwana Marley to do well.

Dan stood there acting excited to go on his hunt, but Marlin clamped down immediately. Professionally and politely he checked out his guest hunter commenting, "Good morning Mister Crowley. I see you are anxious to get underway."

"That I am. Let's get moving."

"First," Marlin continued. "I think you should go and get your hat and perhaps a kerchief because it will be very hot. Is your canteen full? You must have water with you. And don't forget your field glasses. How much ammunition do you have with you?"

Dan continued to play the idiot to the delight of the watching natives. "Oh yes, my hat... field glasses... water..." he replied as he ran off the get his equipment. When he returned, Marlin inspected him again, making sure he actually had water and ammunition. Dan even tried to slip the wrong ammunition past Marlin but was caught. "Mister Crowley, I don't believe this ammunition will work properly in your rifle. Let's get you the right caliber." Then he made sure Dan's rifle was properly loaded and the safety was on before they set off away from the compound.

As they started to walk Marlin could hear a slight metallic sound and immediately knew what Dan was up to. "Mister

Crowley, I believe you have some ammunition clacking together in your pocket. Let's remove that and put those rounds on this belt holder where they won't make noise and will be easy to get to."

Marlin knew a good location to find an Impala but as the idiot hunter, Dan was making noise as he walked and talking too loudly. Marlin politely cautioned him and got him to walk cautiously and quietly. Marlin spotted a nice looking Impala from a distance with the field glasses and explained to Dan exactly how they would get into position to get a shot at the fast moving animal. Finally after a long stalk Marlin had moved his hunter into position.

"Okay Marley," Bwana Dan stated. "You make the shot on this one. Part of this testing is to see if you can hit a live target. It's about a one hundred seventy five yard shot."

Marlin took a prone shooting position and steadied his rifle. He took the safety off and patiently waited for the Impala to give him a side profile shot. He took aim, exhaled slowly and squeezed off the shot. The shot impacted the Impala with a slap and the animal spun in a circle, then bounded off about fifty or sixty yards from where it was hit. It lay down and had its head up. Bwana Dan started to get up off the ground when Marlin stopped him, "Don't move. It's a fatal shot, but he's got to bleed out. If you get up and he sees you, he might run miles before we find him. Let him bleed out, when he puts his head down, he'll be done."

Dan smiled, "You've done very well. Sironka did a good job with you. You even did a good job with my idiot hunter. Looks like his head is down… what do you think?"

"Let's give him another minute or two. He might be trying to fool me too… there's no hurry."

They waited a few more minutes before moving towards the downed Impala. The animal was certainly dead at this point but as they approached, Marlin caught some movement out of the corner of his eye. Bwana Dan was knelt down over the Impala when they heard the sound of a hyena. It was coming at a run towards the downed Impala and Dan. Marlin quickly pulled his rifle to his shoulder and shot the hyena while it was at a full run. The bullet hit the animal, knocking it off its feet and it tumbled head over heels. It managed to crawl off into the brush where it would bleed out and die.

Bwana Dan looked up and proclaimed, "That was a great shot. If you didn't hit him when you did, he might have had me. Damn hyenas. There's probably more of them around but they'll be happy enough to eat the one you shot… but we should probably get out of here."

In the distance they heard some shouting and yelling and then saw Sironka and several of the natives coming their way. They had been monitoring the hunt from a distance watching to see how Bwana Marley did. When he shot the hyena on a dead run there was no containing them. Even the usually stoic Sironka became excited. Soon they were surrounded by the excited natives who quickly gutted the Impala and began to carry it back to the lodge.

Sironka smiled at his friend and simply stated, "Good shot."

*Chapter 18*

# Bunny

M any months passed and Marlin had become a very successful hunting guide. His hunters always did well and Bwana Dan was very pleased with him. He had his own bungalow away from the main lodge and had settled into life in Africa. There were no guest hunters at the lodge and he and Sironka had been out scouting. When he arrived back at the lodge he found Bwana Dan sitting with a tall, sun bronzed man with dark wavy hair. As he entered, Bill called him over, "Marley, come over here. There's a person I want you to meet."

As he approached, Dan began the introduction, "Marley, this is Bunny Allen. He's a hunter from east of here."

Frank M. "Bunny" Allen was a very well-known big game hunter. He was the stereotypical 'Great White Hunter' with his charm and good looks... the complete opposite of the rumpled Dan with his cowboy hat and six-gun. He got the nickname of Bunny as a result of poaching royal game, when as a youngster, he and his gypsy hunting companion would snare rabbits in Winsor forest. He arrived in Kenya in 1927 and quickly established himself as a competent big game hunter and guide.

Bunny put down his drink and extended his hand, "I'm pleased to meet you. Dan has paid you several compliments... especially with regard to your shooting a hyena at a dead run!"

"Thank you. There was a certain degree of luck in that shot but I'm happy to have made it. I've heard a great deal about you as well. You've been out here for a while now."

"Not that long," Bunny replied. "I came out in '27... I'm not an old timer, born and raised here like Dan. I've been told you've done well on your trophy hunts. You must tell me some of your adventures."

"We have had some success," Marlin replied modestly.

"Some success!" interrupted Dan. "He's too modest, he hasn't had an unsuccessful hunt yet. All the clients I have sent him out with have come back happy and they all had something to take back home."

"How about you Marlin?" questioned Bunny. "What trophies have you taken?"

"Actually none... at least not intentionally."

Dan could see where the conversation was moving. The big game hunters of the era marked the measure of a man by how many dangerous animals he killed and while Dan had talked up Marlin, Bunny was curious to see how the young man measured up. Bunny gave him a quizzical look and asked, "None... not even one? How can you be a hunting guide and not kill an animal?"

Marlin was not the same person who left Charleston years before. His time at sea with Captain Mike and his time on the savanna with Sironka had provided him with confidence. He had grown and was modest, yet self-assured enough to not be pushed around by anyone, even a legendary hunter like Bunny Allen.

Marlin answered politely, "There's hunting and there's killing. Every hunt doesn't end in a kill and all kills are not necessarily always the result of a hunt. My job is to get the client into position for a good shot; it's up to him to make the kill. It's also my job to try and get the client back alive... so I have shot a couple of animals."

Bwana Dan interjected, "A couple of animals... that's putting it mildly! There have been at least four hunters who owe their life to this young man and there are a dead lion, leopard, elephant, and water buffalo to prove the point. They may have put the first shot in... or completely missed, but if you hadn't been there to back them up and make that second shot... I hate to think of the outcome."

Marlin didn't respond right away, just took a sip of his drink, and then replied, "I think I'll wash up a bit before dinner. I hope to hear some of Mister Allen's hunting adventures over dinner." He then excused himself and left to get washed up.

Over dinner and several more drinks, Marlin did get to hear stories of Bunny Allen's adventures along with several of Dan's. They were wonderful stories of adventure that could only be told by the men who had lived them. At one point, Bunny asked Marlin, "I'm curious about you young man. You have listened to us… two old hunters telling of our adventures… our philosophy of hunting. I'm curious about your philosophy of hunting. What brought you to Africa and why do you hunt?"

"I came to Africa by chance as a sailor and found that my father had ties to this place. I didn't know that until I arrived here but I had already become fascinated by the vastness and wildness of the place. All the animals… the raw, primitive aspect… I can see how my father was attracted to it. It has helped me to understand him."

"As for the hunting," Marlin thought for a moment before answering, "I enjoy the hunt… the stalk of the prey; the ability to move close to the dangerous animal without his being aware of my presence… trying to think as the animal does and purposely putting myself in the dangerous position. I don't necessarily enjoy the killing of the animal, while sometimes it is required; I take no particular joy in it."

Bunny had more questions, "But what of the trophy? The proof of your conquest… the head on the wall…what of that?"

"I have no need of that. The proof of the conquest is that I'm still alive and not in the belly of the beast. The living of the adventure… the story, that's the most important part. As long as I know the truth, that's all that's important. When I tell the story, the listener can believe it or not… that makes no difference to me. I am content to hunt an animal for the thrill of the hunt and kill it for food... or if it's dangerous rouge, but not for its head."

"So, do you think our hunting clients are fools because they take a trophy?" asked Dan.

"No, not at all, it's a personal choice and they have paid for the privilege. They are brave men looking to face a challenge... maybe face their fear. I don't hold any animosity towards their taking a trophy... a souvenir of the adventure... maybe a once in a lifetime event. But just think of how many animals you've killed over the years. We are out here hunting every day. Sometimes we hunt for food and sometimes for a dangerous rouge animal. If you mounted the heads of all of them... just think... I'll bet you could only get two or three elephant heads plus a lion or two in this room before we would have no room at all. No place left to sit, drink and tell our stories!"

The comment lightened the mood as they envisioned the room full of stuffed heads and since they had been drinking, the laughter came easily. The subject turned to who had the most dangerous hunting client. They spoke of clients who couldn't shoot or accidently discharged the weapon, clients who ran for cover, clients who spooked the animals, but when Dan described the client who when faced by a lion wet himself and climbed a tree, leaving Dan to shoot the beast, the laughter was uncontrollable.

As the evening was winding down, Dan asked Bunny, "So what have you heard from Philip and Blix (Philip Percival and Bron von Blixen-Finecke)... how's the new operation going?"

"They seem to be doing well. The new operation is called Tanganyika Guides Limited and their success rate has been good.

They are both exceptional hunters but Blix is as cynical as ever... women seem to love that about him. You may have heard, they have had a few famous hunters out on safari... the writer, Hemingway was there last summer. Seems all those hunters who shot grisly in America, moose in Canada and tigers in India are all headed to Africa."

Men like Bunny Allen were the ex-patriots of their day, leaving their European homelands in search of fortune, fame and adventure. They were not much different than those that came to Africa to homestead and farm, only they were less settled in their lifestyle. While the farmers came to exploit richness of the land, the big game hunters came to exploit the natural resource of the wild animals. Many of these hunters had been banished to Africa as a result of their financial situation and big game hunting was their last resort. They were a combination of showman, con artist and rogue, selling the African safari and big game hunt as their products.

Bunny took a sip of his drink then became philosophical, directing his wisdom to Marlin, "Enjoy it out here while you can. All this will change someday... it's already changing... might not exist someday... there's already dirt roads cutting back and forth across the savanna. All the European countries want to cut it up... fight over it... divide it... turn it all into farms. Our hunting life is a good way to live but primitive... not just during the day, it's intimate, things happen. A good looking young man like you will find that out soon enough."

Bunny continued giving Marlin a sly smile, "Marlin, just remember there are other kinds of trophies out here... so no matter who you go to bed with, don't tell anyone. If the woman wants to talk about it, that's up to her... it's her reputation."

Marlin didn't really know how to take those words of wisdom, but before long he would find out.

*Chapter 19*

# Sironka

**B**wana Dan had sent Marlin and Sironka to scout for Cape
buffalo, considered by many hunters to be the most dangerous animal in Africa. He had a very rich American arriving in a
few days and wanted to guarantee a good hunt and a grand trophy.
This was the kind of hunter Dan lived for... he was experienced
and wealthy. He would not be a man to back down or make foolish
mistakes. All Dan would have to do is spend a few days in the field
with him and make sure he got his animal.

The two hunters spent several days in locating a group of animals that had the required trophies amongst the herd. As they

walked the two young men spoke very little. They had no need to. There was a bond between them, a respect and understanding. After a time they came to a place on a rise where they could sit and rest for a while and still observe the world around them.

Sironka was the first to speak, "You strange white man, my friend."

Marlin just looked out over the savanna and quietly replied, "How so?"

"You do not look down on black man. You do not try to change us. You show us honor."

Marlin hadn't really given it much thought. "Why should I try to change you? There's nothing wrong with you," he replied.

"White men think we are animals... that we live like animals. They think we have no God."

"We all live like animals," said Marlin. "The white man just hides it from himself better and lies to himself about it. Out here life is much more honest... savage and perhaps even brutal, but honest. Trying to make it civilized, even acting civilized doesn't make it so. White men come out here to hunt to prove they can do what your people have been doing for centuries. They might be more efficient at it because they use guns but that doesn't make them better hunters or more civilized."

"You are better hunter than most white men. Think like animal... track like animal. Better sometimes than me," Sironka commented. "Most white men come to Africa to kill animals... cut heads off to take home, but not you. They want to take our land from us... move us from our home. Why?"

Marlin considered that as a high compliment and replied, "Maybe I'm not as good a hunter as you think... I'm not a better hunter than you. You have killed a lion with a spear while I have used a gun... that makes you the better hunter. As far as your land is concerned... I guess it's because I know I will have to leave Africa one day. Africa to me is like the sea, no one can really own it... it should remain open and free. I guess it's just the nature of man to try and possess land... the tribes here fight over land just like in all other lands.

"You could kill lion with spear," he replied. "But your lion... not live here... live far away."

As Marlin thought about it he realized that Sironka was right. His lion wasn't in Africa, it was back home in Charleston. Someday he would have to face it but he wasn't ready yet. He wondered how Sironka knew. Then he asked him something he had never asked him before, "Tell me about your lion."

Sironka spoke of his preparation to go on the hunt... his preparation for his rite of passage... his fear of failing. As he spoke Marlin realized he was not speaking so much of himself as he was of the lion, the creature he respected and feared. "The lion can run or fight," he said. "My lion would not run. I knew he would not run. My lion would fight. He knew I would not run. I would fight. I did not want to dishonor him. To face the lion you must look into his eyes. The lion has no fear... the lion *is fear!* Even if you fail... even if you die, you face your fear, not die a coward."

They sat for a few more minutes overlooking the vast savanna. "See, my lion will be with me always," he continued as he showed Marlin the scars of the claw marks on his chest while holding the lion claw necklace around his neck. "Wound heals... leaves scar to always remember... some scars are in heart... not seen, only feel those scars."

Marlin thought about his own scars, the death of Mary and abuse by his step-father George... his broken nose, and how he left. His scars were not seen but were still with him. While he had kept in contact with his family, he had recently started to miss them more. Maybe it was because he in some way had connected with the spirit of his father and realized he wasn't a man that would run. He knew he would have to go back and face it all again at some point. It was strange how Sironka, a man living so far away from his life back in the States, could somehow see so deeply into his soul and understand where his fears lay. Facing a wild animal in the heart of Africa wasn't a fear. His fear was facing the condemnation over Mary's death, his responsibility and his abusive step-father.

They sat and looked out over the savanna a while longer before Sironka spoke again, "It is not the same as it was... before white men came. Hunt is different now... now we have guns. Facing the lion now... not close. Takes less courage. Hunters are not the same but lions are the same. These white men who come here... I don't understand. Why do they want the black man's land and his animals?"

"I'll try to explain it to you," Marlin began. "They believe that by killing the biggest, most dangerous animal they prove their bravery and courage... just as you did. They take the head home to show their courage... just as you wear the lion's claws around your neck, wear a headdress and take the tail as a banner. So you see, men of all colors must in some way prove their bravery... prove they are a man. As far as your land... most white men believe they can possess anything. You know better and now I know better... like the animals, we just pass through the land."

"And what happens when all fierce animals are gone?"

"Then they will find another way to prove their courage."

"If they have courage, they should hunt lion with spear," Sironka commented.

"Don't sell them all short. While there's not many, I've met a few who would take up that offer! Some of these men would actually enjoy that challenge!"

"What about you, my white friend... would you face the lion with a spear?"

"I guess I might if I really thought it would prove something to myself, but like you said, my lion doesn't live here."

*Chapter 20*

# Tina

A few days later the wealthy American hunter and his wife arrived. Kenneth and Tina Montgomery were from Hollywood, California. He was a movie producer and she had at one time done some acting until the job of Montgomery's wife became available. Africa had become the fashionable far off exotic destination for many of the wealthy Hollywood crowd. Unlike most of the men who showed up from that group to hunt, Kenneth Montgomery, or 'Monty' as he preferred, was a real big game hunter, although he didn't look the part. He was about fifty-five years old, over weight and balding but an excellent shot and proven big game hunter.

His wife, Tina was at least twenty years younger than Monty. She was a tall, slender, dark haired woman with dark brown eyes and was quite beautiful. The long ride in the truck through the heat of Africa had worn her down. Her hair was a mess and the dust and dirt gave her the appearance that she might have been dragged behind the truck rather than a passenger in it. She looked very displeased and unhappy about the situation. Monty on the other hand was sweating heavily through his safari shirt and covered with dust but had a wide grin of anticipation on his face, clearly happy to be in Africa.

The house staff immediately came running to the truck and took the luggage to their room. The guests attempted to dust themselves off before being escorted to the lodge by Bwana Dan to cool down and have a drink. Marlin observed the arrival but decided to wait a bit before entering the lodge. There was something about the whole thing that put him off so he waited about twenty minutes before going in. When he entered the lodge he found that Dan had supplied everyone with a drink and while Monty looked to be quite comfortable, Tina still looked hot, uncomfortable and irritated. As soon as Marlin entered, Dan began the introductions, "Monty, Tina... this is Marlin... we call him Marley. He is an excellent hunting guide. He's located the herd with your trophy Monty. Marley, this is Ken and Tina Montgomery all the way out here from Hollywood California."

Monty immediately extended his hand, "Good to meet you. Call me Monty. Let's hear about those Cape buffalo."

Marlin shook hands and nodded politely towards Tina, "Good to meet both of you."

Tina perked up a bit and her eyes followed Marlin closely as he went behind the bar and poured himself a drink. Monty was only focused on the Cape buffalo situation and listened closely as Marlin reported to Bwana Dan.

"The herd that Sironka and I located has moved a bit east of where they were yesterday but still near the river. They may be getting some pressure from some lions in the area because they have a few calves in the herd. I don't think they will move much from where they are now."

"Are there some big ones in the group?" asked Monty.

"Yes sir. There are some big bulls with the group. Several fine trophies but it might take a few days of scouting them to get close. They seem to be on edge and that makes them dangerous."

"That's what makes the hunt exciting! The danger in it!" replied Monty.

Marlin had heard this type of bravado all too often, and sometimes found it tiring. In the course of the many dinners he had attended with hunting clients there were often stories of their courage and prowess. Marlin had learned that most couldn't back up their stories in the field. While Bwana Dan encouraged his clients and built up their egos as part of the hunting package, Marlin had discovered over time that there were in fact very few hunters Dan had true respect for. He had even spoken a few times of giving up the hunting guide business but it was usually after having a bad experience with a poor hunter. Marlin didn't make any judgment about Monty since Dan had spoken highly of his abilities. Instead he just announced, "I'll see all of you at dinner, but I must excuse myself now… I have some things to attend to before you go into the field tomorrow."

When Marlin returned to the main house for dinner he found himself seated across the table from Tina. She was now cleaned up and had changed into a sleeveless safari style shirt with the top three buttons conveniently left unbuttoned and a tight pair of slacks. She had an unabashed sexiness about her that she was making no attempt to conceal. It appeared she and Monty had several more cocktails in his absence. Monty was seated across from Dan and was intent on recounting his many hunting adventures. Tina would occasionally roll her eyes as he became more dramatic in his story telling. Marlin listened politely and was aware that Tina was studying him more closely.

Marlin finally broke the silence with her and asked, "Is this your first visit to Africa?"

"Yes," she replied. "Although I don't know what's supposed to be so fascinating about the place. So far all I've seen is herds of filthy animals, dirt and natives."

Marlin continued to be polite, "Well, the country is very beautiful… very wild and untamed. The animals are like no place else in the world."

"That's what I was told. It seems to be all the rage back home to come out here and see it. Now that I'm here I guess I'll just have to make the best of it," she commented as she gave Marlin a very flirtatious smile. "There are some aspects of the country I find interesting."

Monty was completely oblivious to his wife's flirtations seemingly content in his story telling. Dan was acting as the interested host alternating from attentive listener to polite laughter when called for. As the dinner progressed Tina and Monty drank more. She became more flirtatious and Monty became more boisterous. Marlin couldn't believe she was so bold and he was so clueless. He decided it was a good time to excuse himself, pointing out that he would have to be up early to make sure everything was ready for the safari the following day.

Bwana Dan seemed to be tiring of Monty as well and pointed out, "Tomorrow we'll make sure your gun is sighted and ready to go. Then maybe hunt for our dinner. We'll start on safari the day after."

Monty assured Dan he had only one more adventure to relate and then it would be straight to bed. Marlin drifted away from the table leaving Tina pouting, bored by her husband and his story. He went off to his bungalow to get some sleep but the beautiful, flirtatious women stayed on his mind.

The next morning Marlin decided not to have breakfast with Dan and his clients. No matter how you looked at it, Tina was bored and unhappy with her situation... that made her dangerous. Marlin wasn't sure if it was drinking too much or being mad at her husband for dragging her to Africa, but he was very attracted to her and sensed she was trouble... he was going to give her a wide berth. Knowing that breakfast would be over and hearing a rifle being fired out on the range he figured it was a safe time to go to the main house and get a cup of coffee.

As he walked in he greeted the cook, Mbali, a tall, thin, attractive, Zulu woman. Unlike the other natives that worked at the lodge, she was always wearing a dress in the style of an English woman. Her name in Zulu meant 'flower' and it seemed to suit her. She always seemed to have a pleasant smile for everyone... especially Bwana Dan, who she always seemed anxious to please. While it was never spoken about, Marlin understood Mbali was more than just a cook to Dan. Her quarters were attached to the main house and when there were no guests at the lodge to be offended, they shared Dan's bedroom and she took her meals with him. He treated her differently than the others, never speaking a cross or angry word to her. Marlin found her to be interesting... a quiet, gentle, caring person.

"Good morning Mbali. Any coffee left from breakfast?"

"Good morning Bwana Marley... yes we have coffee. Did you sleep well?"

Marlin poured himself a cup and looked out the window. It looked like it would be a reasonably mild day. "Yes, I slept very well. Did they go down to the rifle range?" he asked.

"The man he go with Bwana Dan. Lady leave later. Go for walk."

Marlin drank the last of his coffee and set his cup down. "Do you know where she went to walk?"

"No," Mbali answered. "She very unhappy woman. Not happy in Africa."

An unsettling feeling came over Marlin. Africa wasn't the kind of place you just go for a walk, especially if you were unprepared for what you might find... or what might find you. No one except the natives ever walked away from the hunting lodge without a rifle. Marlin walked over to the gun rack and pulled down a rifle, checked to see that it was loaded and then went outside to see if he could track Tina down. It wasn't long before he found her footprints and began to follow her. It took about twenty minutes to catch up to her and it appeared she had lost the marked trail she had started out on. It was a good sign she was lost. He came over a rise and she was now just about forty yards ahead of him. What she didn't see was a young lioness less than one hundred yards away that was watching her.

Marlin didn't yell he just stated in a firm voice, "Tina, stop right where you are... don't turn around. Hold still. Perfectly still... there's a lion directly in front of you."

Tina was lost and the sound of Marlin's voice was a great relief. She started to turn around and this time he was more forceful, "Damn it! I said don't turn around!"

At that point, the lioness slowly walked into view. She was standing erect, not crouched or acting like she was stalking, but she was clearly interested. Tina now saw the lion and while she wanted to run, she was frozen with fear.

Marlin was now thinking about if he would have to shoot the lion but Tina was directly in his line of fire. If she charged he'd have to chance it. He slowly walked towards Tina and spoke to her as he moved, "Don't turn away from her and don't run. She'll have you before I might get a shot off. Just don't move."

Tina instinctively started to back away. "Don't move!" Marlin demanded. "I'm almost behind you."

As he got to where Tina was standing he stated again as he touched her shoulder, "Don't move. She hasn't made her decision yet," Marlin stated as he raised the rifle to his shoulder.

"Shoot it!" Tina demanded as the lioness took a few more tentative steps towards them.

"Not yet. She's not all that interested in you anymore now that I'm here. She's just a bit curious. You don't smell like the food she's used to. Give her a moment."

The big cat stood and looked at Tina with big yellow eyes for a few more moments but no longer advanced. She had the look of a curious house cat on her face, just looking over the situation and trying to figure it out. The lioness gave a big yawn, showing her huge teeth and Tina gasped. Marlin commented, "She's bored with you now. You're not interesting to her anymore. She'll leave in a moment or two."

Then the lioness casually walked off and disappeared into the bush like a tan ghost. Tina turned quickly now burying her face into Marlin's chest, wrapped her arms around him and started to cry. It was a cry as much of relief as fear. While he liked the feeling of her in his arms he still pushed her away, "There's no need to cry. Besides, we need to get out of here. She might not be interested in us right now or she might be getting the rest of her pride so they can enjoy an easy meal."

It was about ten minutes before they reached the area where Tina had lost the trail and become lost. "Here's where you went wrong," Marlin pointed out. "The trail goes this way, see the animal tracks, they use the same trail as us... but you went wrong long before that."

"What do you mean?" she asked.

"Never go off walking out here unarmed or by yourself. In your case, just never go walking without an armed guard. Being on a trail doesn't make you any safer than being off the trail. The lions know other animals use the trail. If I hadn't arrived when I did that lion would have had you. She might not even be hungry; it just would have been too easy for her to pass up."

"But I didn't even see her. How did you see her?"

"First, she was counting on you not seeing her. Second, I always anticipate that there will be a lion hiding in the bush so I'm looking for them. She only came out because you stopped coming towards her. Then she wanted to see if you would run. If you ran then you were prey but when you didn't she wasn't sure what you were… she still knew you were food, she just wasn't sure what type or if you would be good to eat."

"Why didn't you shoot her?" Tina demanded.

"I didn't have to. We had a standoff today. I didn't shoot her just for being a lion, and she didn't eat you just for being foolish… that seems fair."

On the way back Tina started to walk rapidly, anxious to get back to safety. Marlin quickly stopped her. "Stop," he ordered. "Out here we move cautiously. Watch where you walk. There are not just lions out here that can kill you, there are several types of poisonous snakes. This trail is narrow, the perfect place for small game to travel. The snake lies in wait for something to come by and strikes. If they feel the vibration of something big coming, they don't want to get trampled and move away. Since we're not that big they might not know we're coming right away. Move to fast and you might be on them quickly… too close, they panic and strike."

They were now back at the lodge and the rifle fire could still be heard. "Your husband should almost be done sighting in his rifle. He should be back shortly, then they will be off to hunt for dinner. You'll have to excuse me, I have some work to attend to." Marlin walked off with his rifle slung over his shoulder leaving Tina standing in front of the lodge.

*Chapter 21*

# Trophy

It was mid-morning when Monty and Bwana Dan arrived back at the lodge. They were both satisfied that the rifle was set up properly for Monty and he would be able to hit his target. Tina made no mention of her encounter with the lion and just listened to Monty brag about how well he shot at the range. Monty was anxious for some action and wanted no more than to get into the field and shoot something.

"Well Dan, what do you think? Ready to go out and do some hunting?" asked Monty.

"Indeed, yes!" Dan answered. "Why don't we take the rest of the morning and afternoon? We'll go out and bag a couple of animals... bring back something for dinner. We'll take a couple of boys with us. We'll leave tomorrow for your safari to get that Cape buffalo. Marley will be taking care of the last details today."

Tina took notice that they would be gone all the rest of the day but was especially interested in the fact Marlin would not be going with them. She politely sat and had a cup of coffee with them before they left and even acted interested in their hunt. She waited until they had left and then went to her room to get ready for her hunt. She cleaned up and changed into clean clothes. She fussed with her hair a bit and then dabbed on a touch of perfume before she went out to see where Marlin was.

Marlin had given all the last minute instructions to the safari bearers. Most of the work had been done previously and while Dan felt they needed constant supervision, Marlin had learned that the bearers prepared for safari so many times, they needed little supervision. He went back to his bungalow to pack what he would need for the hunt and to clean his rifle. He was only there a few moments when there was a knock at the door.

He had removed his shirt and had his back to the door. He was washing his face when he heard the knock and expected it was one of the bearers with a question. "Come in," he responded while he was wiping off the water off, his face buried in a towel. He heard the door close as he turned around, removing the towel from his face, he found Tina standing in his room.

He was caught off guard, "Oh, I didn't know it was you. Is there something I can do for you?"

"I came by to properly thank you for saving my life from that lion," she replied as she moved closer. "If it wasn't for you, I wouldn't be here." Then she casually put her arms around his neck and gave him a long kiss.

Marlin was lost in that kiss for a moment before realizing that he was kissing a married woman. His sensibilities took hold for an instant and he asked, "What about your husband?"

She kissed him again and started to unbutton the last few buttons of her half unbuttoned shirt. "You've seen my husband. He's old and boring. All he wants to do is shoot some dirty old animals to prove he's manly. We've been married for ten years... back then he had hair and wasn't so fat... back then he could take care of my needs."

"Then why do you stay with him?" he asked.

"He has lots of money. He's going to kill himself trying to prove he's a great hunter. He'll either drop dead from a heart attack or one of those filthy animals will kill him and all that money will be left to me... I've made sure of that! Don't get me wrong. I like Monty... I think I even loved him at one time but now he just brings me along as another testimony to his virility. People see him with a younger woman and they think he must be man enough to please her... at least that's what he believes."

By this time her shirt was off and she pressed her bare breasts up against Marlin's chest. Her perfume was intoxicating and he now found himself pulling her close... his moral dilemma over Monty was fading. She kissed him again and the moral dilemma within him vanished completely. He briefly had a vision of an angry Monty bursting in and shooting him dead on the spot but that was quickly forgotten as he felt her undo his pants. She let her dark hair down and gave her head a little shake allowing it to fall over her bare shoulders.

Tina gave Marlin a mischievous smile and continued her comments, "Don't worry about my husband... let's concentrate on sexual desire. Back home this kind of thing happens all the time... we just have to be discrete. Just remember, it's my vacation, too! I want a trophy from my visit to Africa! Besides, I've seen the way you've been looking at me... you want me as much as I want you."

The words of Bunny Allen came back into his head, but by this time Marlin had already decided that whatever was going to happen he was on board with it. Within a minute she had her pants off and they were in bed, her seduction almost complete. She knew what she wanted and was not shy about it.

As they started to make love she whispered in Marlin's ear, "Harder... you won't break me. Take me like one of your savage wild animals."

When they were done they lay in bed coming back to their senses. There was no doubt about it, Tina was skilled. She cuddled up to him and kept him just on edge until she knew he was ready to perform again. Then she rolled on top of him and demanded, "One more time before I have to leave."

This time when they were done they were both completely spent and lay there like rag dolls. As he lay there, Marlin couldn't help but think that if Monty came through the door at that instant he couldn't even run, he would be shot as he lay in bed. His entire body had been sapped of its strength and he didn't care. It was about twenty minutes before they could get dressed. After they dressed, Tina gave him a long kiss good bye and then said, "Thanks. That was the best part of my trip so far. We may have to do it again before I leave."

Tina went back to the lodge to un-ruffle herself after rolling around in Marlin's bed and Marlin went back to checking on the safari preparations. He was surprised to find he didn't feel any remorse or shame for bedding a married woman. He wondered if that would change when he was face to face with her husband. The thought of him being an African trophy crossed his mind and he laughed to himself. Was he the trophy or was she? He guessed it could go both ways. The idea of becoming a trophy without giving up your life or your head did have a certain appeal in it… and of course there was the physical gratification. Tina seemed so matter of fact about it all; just an amusement, something to keep her from excessive boredom. He could even see her side of the issue. Monty had this beautiful, sexy woman who he paid no attention to… it just didn't seem right.

That evening at dinner Monty drank and told stories of his day on the hunt. It was a repeat of the previous night except Tina seemed to flirt a little less and had a smug, satisfied look on her face. Bwana Dan was the perfect host as always and Marlin tried to seem interested in the events of the day. A couple of times Tina stretched her foot out under the table and rubbed it against Marlin's leg, giving him a half smile in the process. He could tell that she was just trying to live a little dangerously by doing it right in front of her unsuspecting husband. She had a few more drinks and Marlin sensed that it was time to excuse himself before the drinks made her too brazen.

"I'm afraid I must excuse myself a bit early this evening," he announced. "There's always a few last minute details that need checking before we go on safari. Want to make sure we have everything we need to get Monty that buffalo."

"Excellent," Monty exclaimed. "I can't wait to find that big fellow and take him."

Tina gave him a look of distress as he left her alone with Dan and her husband. He went back to his bungalow, closed the door, and this time he locked it. There was no telling what Tina might be up to and it would be a good idea to get some distance from her... he figured he tempted fate enough for one day. As he cleaned his gun in preparation for the safari it occurred to him that while she might be beautiful and the sex was great, Tina was no bargain herself. She and Monty might actually be just made for each other... her waiting for him to die and him boring her to death in the process. At the same time, he enjoyed the experience of bedding her and if the opportunity came his way again, he had no doubt he would do it again... but like Bunny told him, he would not speak of it to anyone.

*Chapter 22*

# Kudo

The African Cape Buffalo has a reputation as a mean, ornery, unpredictable and highly dangerous animal for a good reason. The males can weigh from eleven to two thousand pounds and have massive horns that are fused at their base... bullets can't always penetrate through the base and reach the animal's brain. Taking one down before it takes you down requires expert shot placement and the need to get close. Lions in a group will attack a cape buffalo but rarely a full size male, usually a weaker member of the heard or a calf. A lone lion would never take on a healthy, full size male... so if a lion won't take them on, there's not any other animal that will.

The tribal people are cautious if not fearful of the Cape buffalo. Like the lion, hippo or crocodile it is responsible for just as many deaths to humans. Those who hunt them for sport put their lives on the line in the process. Monty had set his sights on taking one of these animals and Marlin believed from the standpoint of his shooting he was fully capable. He was an excellent shot with a rifle but was not in particularly good physical shape. He would be subject to over exertion and if he had to move fast to get out of an animal's way, he would be in serious trouble.

It was just before sunrise when the native bearers and Marlin set off into the bush carrying all the supplies that would be needed to set up a comfortable camp. They would not reach their destination for two days. In the meantime, Bwana Dan, Monty and Tina would stay at the compound. They would later travel by truck with a few native bearers as far as they could and then walk in the last five miles... something Tina was not looking forward to.

When they arrived at their destination, the camp was set up. Bwana Dan tried to provide the most comfortable of settings for his hunters and while they were in the middle of nowhere, he tried to provide all the comforts of home. Clients like Monty and Tina wanted the camping experience in the wilds of Africa as long as good food, clean beds and cocktails were provided. There were separate tents for Bwana Dan, Marlin, Monty and Tina. There was a cook tent to keep food and supplies plus an open air cooking station. Bwana Dan made sure that there was also a small shower tent so at the end of a long dirty day the guest could clean up before cocktails were served. A large dining table was located near a campfire which was constantly attended to... not necessarily for heat, but to keep animals from visiting the camp. Location of the camp was critical since it was out where any number of animals could just walk through and sometimes did. It was a location they had used many times, away from most heavily used games trails... close to water, but not too close.

During the day the camp was a busy, active place but at night when the darkness surrounded it was when Marlin found it to be the most beautiful. Not being able to see past the edge of camp, the sounds of the animals somewhere out there just beyond where they could be seen, the stars shining in the black sky and only the glow of the campfire made the safari camp a mix of beauty and danger that was irresistible to Marlin. Sitting at the table or around the camp-fire, having a drink and listening to the stories was the best part. It seemed that even Monty's stories would be relevant in that setting.

Bwana Dan, Monty and Tina arrived just before noon. Bwana Dan looked like he had just been for a walk in a park wearing his dirty cowboy hat, his forty five on his hip and carrying a rifle. Monty looked worn out, sweating heavily but smiling and looking happy to be in camp. Tina just looked miserable. Hiking through the bush in the heat of Africa was not to her liking but she believed that in order to eventually get Monty's money she needed to stay close and play along.

"Welcome to camp," Marlin greeted them.

"It looks fine, well done," replied Bwana Dan.

Monty shook Marlin's hand and commented, "This is top notch! Beautiful location! Have you seen much game about?"

"There's plenty of game around," Marlin replied. "I haven't seen any buffalo yet... but I don't think you'd want to see them here in camp would you?"

"No indeed! They'd make quite a mess of things, wouldn't they?" Monty replied with a hearty laugh. "We'll find them soon enough!"

"How did you enjoy your little hike to camp?" Marlin asked Tina, knowing full well that she absolutely hated it.

"Oh, it was quite lovely if you like dirt, heat and the possibility of being eaten alive at any moment," she replied sarcastically. "I assume this is as close to civilization as I will find out here in the middle of nowhere."

Marlin found it hard not to laugh at her situation and just politely replied, "Yes, this is it. As a camp goes, it is more civilized than most. You have your own tent, someone will cook your meals, we have a shower so you can clean up… you might find the toilet facilities a bit rustic. We're off the main game trails, but I wouldn't wander out of camp if I were you."

As he pointed to her tent he continued, "That tent is yours. The shower is over there. When you want water to shower, just ask one of the boys and they'll bring you some water. The river is about a half mile from here. Don't go there… hippos and crocs, plus you never know what might stop by for a drink!"

Now that she had seen her safari home, Tina stomped off to her tent. Marlin had seen a small smile come over Monty's face as Tina stomped off. He acted completely unfazed by her misery but Marlin sensed that he actually was enjoying it.

"So, what's for dinner?" asked Bwana Dan.

"Nothing yet. I haven't gone hunting. There's plenty around here within a short distance. Perhaps after a short rest, Monty might like to take a walk with me and shoot our dinner."

"That's a great idea!" Monty chimed in. "I'd love to shoot something and Dan tells me you're an excellent tracker. Maybe I'll learn something along the way."

It was about an hour and a half later that Marlin and Monty left camp to hunt for dinner. They walked at a slow pace and Monty studied everything that Marlin was doing. After they had gone about a quarter mile, Monty asked, "I hope you're not traveling so slow on my account?"

"Not at all. I know Bwana Dan sometimes moves more quickly than I do, but I've found that moving more slowly works best for me. I'll move a bit then stop, look, listen... see what's around... see what might be looking at me. If you move too fast, you might miss a sign or a track. For instance, those tracks there were made by a kudu... he's good sized and he's not too far away. With some luck, he might be our dinner."

Monty took it all in and was impressed. They moved a bit further and Marlin stopped again. He pointed out some more tracks. "We're close now he whispered. See how defined the tracks are... no damage from wind... the dirt on the edge is sharp. Your Kudu will be very close now but the wind is changing so we'll approach him from another direction... follow me."

They moved off in a slightly different direction and Marlin had Monty settle down and get ready to shoot. "The Kudu will move through this area in a few minutes," he whispered. There will be several small ones and at least one of good size... that's the one you want. We have lots of people to feed tonight. Stay alert... there were leopard tracks back there as well. He's looking for dinner, too."

About five minutes went by and some animals came into view. They were moving into a brush area where they would be less visible to predators. Marlin put his hand on Monty's shoulder and whispered, "Kudus will stay close to the brush or hillsides. They don't like being in the open. They're not as fast as other antelope species. They will have to move across that open spot. Here comes a big one. Let him move in about twenty five more yards or so and take your shot. It's about one hundred yards… our wind is okay… he won't know what hit him."

Monty took the rifle off safe, balanced the gun and waited. Marlin observed Monty and it was clear he knew what he was doing. He was calm as the Kudu walked into range just as Marlin said it would. Monty took aim, exhaled as he squeezed off the shot. The shot was perfect. The Kudu jerked back and moved about thirty yards. The massive damage to its lungs caused the animal to be unable to breathe and it lay down as all the other animals ran. Marlin congratulated Monty on a fine shot, "Well done, dinner and a respectable trophy. We'll wait a few minutes until he bleeds out then move up on him and wait. Some of the boys will be here shortly."

"How do you know that?" asked Monty.

"They heard the shot so they know dinner is served… or it will be after they gut the animal and haul it back. We're no more than a mile from camp. I told them about where we'd be. The leopard will have to find dinner elsewhere."

They went down and looked over the Kudu. It had a fine set of spiral horns and was a much bigger, better looking animal than Marlin expected. Monty was overjoyed, "I didn't expect we'd be getting such a fine trophy animal on a meat hunt! You are quite a hunter. It's almost as if you knew exactly where the animal would walk."

Marlin explained modestly, "I did know where he would go... or where I expected him to go. That type of animal isn't comfortable where he was located. He wants to be in a more covered area where it's not so easy to be ambushed. I knew he would eventually move towards deeper cover in the afternoon. Since he was heading that way and we hadn't spooked him it was just a matter of waiting until he showed. It would have all changed if that leopard had spooked him before we got our chance. If that happened he would have run past us before we ever got into position and we might not have ever seen him."

"What about the leopard?"

"The leopard? He's gone. He was ahead of us... probably had the same plan to ambush an animal... might have even been watching us. They're very elusive, but now that we're here and took his dinner, he's left."

A group of native bearers arrived from the camp and set about getting the animal back to camp. Marlin told them to give the cook the backstrap of the animal and the remainder was theirs, except the horns which would be kept a trophy. On the way back to camp they walked at a leisurely pace and Monty began to talk. He was passionate about hunting and loved being out in the bush.

"I envy you Marlin," he commented. "I envy your youth and your hunting skills. I took up hunting later in life and regret the time I lost. I'm so grateful for every adventure I have out here. This all may be gone someday."

"I don't think your wife shares your love of the outdoors."

Monty laughed and continued, "No, she hates it out here. I only bring her along to piss her off. When we first got married things were pretty good; she was lots of fun, but after a while I found we only had one thing in common... my money. I'm a very wealthy man. I've made lots of money in the movie business and that's why she won't leave me."

Marlin was wondering how much Monty knew. He wasn't stupid and Marlin was finding that he liked Monty. At least there was something he was passionate about and he liked the fact he was onto his wife.

"My health isn't what it used to be," Monty continued. "I've tried to take better care of myself, but my doctors tell me that even with that I might only get another ten years or so. I'd like to prove them all wrong, but it seems they probably know what they're talking about... they usually do. They told me this type of physical activity is good for me, so I'll continue to hunt and be active as long as I can. Tina thinks there's going to be a big payoff for her in the end. She'll get something of course, but not as much as she thinks she will. I'm in the process of spending my money... travel, hunting trips, that kind of stuff. She thinks there is a never ending pile of loot! So she can come along and have fun or sit on the sidelines, pout and be miserable... doesn't matter to me. She's a realist as well. The only reason she forces herself to come on these trips is to make sure no one cuts in on her action. Back in Hollywood there's lots and lots of beautiful women as you would imagine. Women like Tina always have strings attached... after a while sometimes they just become a pain in the ass!"

"So what do you do about that?" asked Marlin.

"Even as old and beat up as I am, I could divorce her and replace her easily. After all, I'm the one who has the money. The problem is that her replacement might end up being a bigger pain in the ass than she is, so I'll keep her around. As they say, better the devil you know! But it's a good lesson for a young man like you… make sure if you get married that the woman has a heart!"

By the time they got back to camp everything was set up for dinner. Monty got cleaned up and as soon as Marlin made sure the cook had received the Kudo meat he readied himself as well. Dining out on the savanna was one of the highlights of every safari and something Marlin always looked forward to. It was as if they were performing a highly civilized ritual in the most primitive location on earth. As the sun set, cocktails were served. Fires were set at the perimeter of the camp causing a glow as the stars came out. The cook took great pride in presenting an outstanding meal and Bwana Dan made for the perfect host. Cigars were smoked and stories were told… often becoming more interesting as more alcohol was consumed. In the darkness you could hear the sounds of the night animals all around you.

Marlin could see that Tina was not enjoying the situation. She did not find any beauty in the African surroundings. She sat at her end of the table drinking and looking quite bored by it all. Occasionally she would give Marlin a look and send a smile his way. Monty however was thoroughly enjoying himself, enjoying his drinks and telling his stories.

After a while, Marlin excused himself and went to his tent leaving the unhappy Tina to fend for herself. He went in, checked around as he always did for any unwelcome crawling guests, got into his bed and quickly put out the light. He was thankful Tina had the good sense and discretion not to follow him. His thoughts turned to Bunny Allen and his advice. While he did feel a slight sense of guilt, he did not feel a bit of regret. Tina, he believed, felt neither a sense of guilt or regret.

*Chapter 23*

# Cape Buffalo

**B**wana Dan, Monty and two bearers left before sunrise to search out some Cape buffalo. It would then take several hours to reach the area where they expected the buffalo to be and if they shot one they would not be back until late in the day. Marlin went about organizing the remaining bearers to get their daily chores done. They would need wood for a fire and cooking, water for cleaning up, and general camp maintenance. The hunters were long gone by the time Tina finally got up. She made her way to where the coffee was and the camp cook, Andre, poured her a cup. Andre was the safari cook. His name was unpronounceable by most English speakers so everyone called him Andre. Mbali never came on safari. Tina walked back to her tent, sat in a chair, slowly sipping her coffee and looking over the camp, searching for Marlin.

He came walking back into camp from the outskirts, rifle slung over his shoulder wearing his khaki shirt and pants, wide brimmed hat with leopard skin band... looking every inch the young, dashing, great white hunter. He got a cup of coffee, walked over and acknowledged Tina, "Good morning. Sleep well?"

"I slept alone," she replied with a bit of a pout. "So I could have slept better. The great hunter is off looking for a stupid buffalo?"

"Yeah, they left about two hours ago."

"Will they get any?"

"Oh, I expect they'll find some, there's lots of buffalo out here and we know where they'll be. Monty's a good shot. If Dan can get him in position he'll get his buffalo... or the buffalo might get him, there's no guarantee with buffalo."

"Please, sit down," Tina invited as she motioned to a chair.

Marlin took the rifle off his shoulder and sat down. Tina looked beautiful... a little unkempt and wild, but beautiful. She smiled at him... a dangerous, flirtatious smile. "Marley," she began. "I think I would like nothing better this morning than for you to come into my tent, undress me slowly, and then make love to me."

Marlin didn't answer which was all the encouragement she needed. She took him by the hand and they entered the tent. Once inside he set the rifle down and she immediately began kissing him passionately. He started undressing her and she slowed him down whispering to him, "Take your time. Think of it as slowly unwrapping a present… explore me with your hands."

Before long they were in bed getting down to business and Tina mentioned, "We will be leaving soon to return home. I want to leave you with a memory of making love in a tent in the middle of the African savanna… I want you look back on this moment warmly years from now… I'm going to make sure you remember me… and I trust you will do your best to make sure I remember you."

Meanwhile, Monty was being guided to an area where a herd of Cape buffalo had been seen previously. Bwana Dan had guided him to a spot where they could glass an area to spot them and plan their stalk. A small herd was located in a wooded area shading themselves under a few small trees. They seemed to be resting comfortably and there was adequate cover for the hunting party to approach from downwind. There were at least two large trophy bulls in the group that were visible.

As they began to move towards the buffalo they used the high grass for cover. The buffalo could be approached and they could get close provided they did not become aware of the hunters presence. When they were about halfway to their prey, Bwana Dan and Monty did a last check on their weapons to make sure they were loaded and ready for action. While both hunters were sure they were ready, the last check was done more as a self confidence boost and gut check before you confronted one of the largest, most deadly animals on the face of the earth. Both men were ready and made their move to cover the last fifty yards. The native bearers would stay at a safe distance far away from them. They slowly moved forward keeping a close watch on the buffalo. They knew at some point the buffalo would see them… there were too many of them… too many eyes not to see them at some point, but their sense of smell is better than their eyesight. If they saw something they might move around a bit but wouldn't necessarily panic and become aggressive, but if there was a scent attached to what they saw they would become defensive quickly.

The hunters were now within about forty yards of their target. Bwana Dan whispered to Monty, "See that big boy off to the left… that's your trophy. What do you think?"

"Oh yeah, he's a big one! We'll have to move off to the left to get a clear shot. I don't want to risk shooting through the trees."

"Okay," replied Dan. "Slowly move off to your left… I'll stay behind you and to your right."

At that point a few of the buffalo had noticed the men and had stood up. Since the men were now moving away to the left of the herd they didn't seem too concerned. Most animals move away when Cape buffalo are in their path. A few trotted away but most didn't move much. Then Bwana Dan felt the one thing he dreaded… he felt a breeze suddenly on his neck.

"The wind is changing," he whispered to Monty. "Take your shot."

No sooner than the words left his lips, all the buffalo were on their feet. Several snorted and started to trot off. The large bull was now facing the hunters and slowly moving towards them thinking about if he would charge the intruders. Monty knew he didn't have a shot. Shooting the bull in the head wouldn't take him down, he needed a shot to the heart and lungs. The bull turned sharply and moved to the right of the hunters. It was a broadside shot, just what

Monty needed but there were now some trees between him and the bull. There were other buffalo moving more quickly now becoming agitated and aggressive. The large bull was now moving closer directly towards them and the broadside shot was gone. Bwana Dan was looking for a place to move Monty for cover but there wasn't anything available. They were completely exposed now and there was no going back.

The large bull turned again presenting a broadside shot. There was a small gap between the trees providing a clear shot for a brief moment if the bull kept moving. The other buffalo were now highly agitated and about ready to run. The bull moved and Monty held his ground. Then in a brief instant he was presented with his shot. Monty quickly took aim and squeezed the trigger. The loud explosion of the rifle blast panicked the buffalo and they scattered in all directions, some directly at the two hunters. Both hunters dove towards some small trees to avoid being run over by the buffalo. Bwana Dan was lucky, the buffalo missed him but Monty didn't do so well. A buffalo had struck him with a glancing blow as it ran past, knocking him down onto a large rock. Dan ran over to him as the buffalo cleared out from the area.

"Monty... are you okay?"

Monty was shook up and battered but conscious, "I think I broke my arm."

"How do you know?"

"I heard it snap," Monty replied weakly. "Did I get him?"

"I don't know... I think so," Bwana Dan replied. "Let me help you up and we'll see."

Dan helped Monty to his feet, and picked up his rifle. The native bearers were now on scene pointing excitedly towards a spot past where they last saw the large male buffalo. Dan quickly fashioned a sling for Monty's arm with his bandana and they moved to where they thought the buffalo might be. When they found the buffalo he was down but still alive so they couldn't approach. A wounded buffalo can be more dangerous than a healthy buffalo, especially if it can still get to its feet! Dan was getting ready to put another shot into the animal when Monty stopped him, "Don't shoot. I want to finish it."

"Are you sure? What about your arm?"

"It's my left arm that's broke... I can still use my right. I'll prop my rifle on this tree limb and put one shot in his spine... just work the action... load it for me."

Monty worked through the pain and balanced the rifle on the tree limb and shot the buffalo in the spine, putting him down. Bwana Dan took the rifle and congratulated him, "Fine work... that's a trophy to be proud of. Sorry about your arm. It's going to be a long walk back but I'll send one of the boys ahead to get some help and leave one here to protect your buffalo until we can get some help."

Back at the camp, Tina and Marlin had finished making memories and were lying together regaining their composure. Marlin finally got up and dressed and went back outside. Tina took a while longer to put herself back together. It was a few hours later when the native runner came into camp with the news of Monty's injury. Marlin quickly left with several bearers to meet the hunters on their way back.

Bwana Dan and Monty had walked for less than an hour when Dan decided it was as far as he wanted Monty to go. They were still far from camp so he found a shady spot and made Monty comfortable. They hadn't made much progress and it had been slow going. Monty was out of breath, sweating profusely in the heat and was very uncomfortable but was still upbeat and willing to continue. He was still on a high from the hunt.

"I can keep going, there's no need to stop."

"We'll stop," replied Dan. "Take a drink of water and put this wet rag on your head. Help should get here in a few hours. We'll wait here, cool down and relax. How's the arm?"

"It hurts... but it would hurt more if I missed that buffalo. That was quite a hunt... a real adventure... it would make a hell of a movie."

Dan reached into his pack and pulled out a bottle, "I'm not much of a doctor, but I believe we can help your pain a bit with this."

"Hey, were you holding out? I could have used that a couple of hours ago before we started this hike."

"I figured that a man with a broken arm was enough to contend with... a drunk man with a broken arm would be too much... couldn't have you stumbling around out here. Besides, I figured we'd stop at some point and wait for help. We can drink and tell stories while we wait. Here, take a drink."

He passed the bottle to Monty and the two old hunters drank and told stories until the rescue party arrived. When Marlin finally got to them he yelled a greeting as he approached, "Help has arrived!"

"Good to see you Marley," Dan responded. "Monty has a broken arm that will need medical attention. The bone hasn't broken through the skin but he'll have to have it set and fixed up by a real doctor."

"I brought the medical kit. We should get it stabilized a bit better before we move him any further... maybe that will reduce the pain."

"I'm pretty sure I've taken care of the pain issue," Dan commented with a smile.

"I'm feeling much better now than I did a while ago," Monty chimed in, his speech slightly slurred. "But I'm sure that's the medicinal whiskey doing its work. Marley, you should have been there... what an adventure... well worth having a broken arm!"

"I'm anxious to hear about it," he replied, thinking for a moment of his own adventure with Tina. "We're going to use a litter to carry you back to camp and you can tell me on the way."

"Oh, I won't need that! I can make it back under my own power," Monty protested as he tried to get up. The whiskey had taken its toll on the wounded hunter and he quickly found he was not able to move to his feet. "Well, maybe not," he said as he reconsidered his situation. "It seems Bwana Dan's doctoring has gotten me drunk. What a great story this will make! Hunting the Cape buffalo... almost getting killed... getting drunk in the middle of Africa and getting hauled back to camp, too wounded, drunk and happy to walk! Hell, it might make a great movie!"

*Chapter 24*

# Monty's Farewell

It was early evening by the time the hunters returned to the safari camp with the injured Monty. By that time the whiskey had worn off and he was in some pain but he was still excited about his hunt and would talk about it to anyone who would listen. Tina showed a proper amount of compassion for her wounded husband but didn't overdue it. Marlin couldn't help but think that she might have been a very successful actress if she had not given up her career.

Marlin had the native bearers start to make preparations to break camp for an early morning start back to the lodge. It might be several days before Monty would be able to see a doctor and get his arm set. Monty wasn't overjoyed at having to cut his safari adventure short but as whiskey wore off and the pain set in he could see there was really no choice. After a good meal and several drinks he was still a bit uncomfortable but in better spirits.

Monty raised his glass in a toast to his hunting guides, "To Dan and Marley... this has truly been a wonderful adventure. I've had a splendid time here in Africa. I wouldn't have missed it for the world... even with the broken arm. I want the both of you to know that while I have to cut my hunt short, I will still be paying the complete fee plus a generous tip for you two and I hope to come back here and hunt again."

Tina squirmed a little in her chair. While she had bagged her trophy in Africa she didn't want to pay a trophy fee. She was more than ready to go home and she hated seeing Monty spend what she considered her money. Marlin gave some thought to what Monty would do when he got back to Hollywood. He figured as soon as his arm healed and he could get back to hunting he would be off on another adventure. He would stick with his plan to live out his dreams and spend his fortune. Maybe Tina would get wise to his plan... maybe she wouldn't. If she figured it out she would be gone but Marlin figured she probably wouldn't get wise too soon.

Marlin had a restless night's sleep. He had a dream about Mary. His life in Charleston seemed like it was so long ago. He had pushed it to the back of his mind while at sea on the *Shamrock Isle* and while he was so far away in Africa. He had feelings for Mary and with the women he had been with since, it was purely physical. It was a part of him he had come to accept. There was no commitment, it was fun and he enjoyed it. It was just part of being human. He was still unsure about all that had happened surrounding Mary's death. Had he in some way been responsible? He hadn't been drinking, but what if they didn't run away? Would they have had a life together? Would they have been kept apart? She would still be alive but with someone else? Would he ever find someone like her again? Then Tina crept into his dreams. She would indeed leave him with some lasting memories but he also felt some guilt. Bunny Allen never said anything about guilt... maybe Bunny never felt guilty. He did say it was the woman's problem, not his and he didn't seem to be a man who lived with guilt. He seemed to be more of a man who lived in the moment taking whatever came his way. Maybe it was because Marlin liked Monty... he got to know him and in many ways respected him.

It was early the next morning when they broke camp and headed back home. Monty and Tina would spend one last night at the hunting lodge before returning to civilization. There would be one last dinner and this time Marlin spent the time listening to Monty's stories and found himself enjoying them. Tina left early to go off to bed when she didn't receive the attention she desired. Marlin felt that there was something fatalistic in Monty. He seemed to be trying to get as much living in as he could in a short time. He got the distinct impression that maybe Monty didn't have all that much time to live and somehow he knew it. He seemed to hint at it when they hunted for the Kudu. He wondered how he would react if he were in the same situation. He had to have some level of fear facing his own mortality. Would he have the guts that this overweight, middle aged man from Hollywood had? Could he learn something from Monty and apply it to his own life? Bwana Dan, Marlin and Monty drank, told stories and enjoyed each other's company long into that last night.

## Chapter 25

# The Zebra Story

Several days had passed since Monty and Tina left. Marlin came into the lodge and entered the dining area where he found Dan and Mbali seated eating breakfast. As soon as she realized Marlin was in the room she started to rise out of her chair to leave.

"No," Marlin stated. "Please stay seated… don't get up. Finish your food."

She looked at Dan for direction knowing her being seated at the same table was considered taboo. Dan looked at Marlin and then back at Mbali, then just nodded to her to sit back down. He knew that Marlin didn't care and was not passing any judgment. He felt a certain sense of relief along with a level of comfort.

"You've got a lot of your father in you. This wouldn't have bothered him either."

Marlin poured himself a cup of coffee and then sat at the table. Mbali seemed a bit confused and a little uneasy in the situation. Marlin didn't comment, he just smiled at Mbali and commented, "Good coffee."

After that they sat at the table and spoke as any other people would over coffee and Mbali began to feel at ease. Marlin found Mbali to be fascinating in her own way. She was from the Zulu tribe, about thirty or thirty five, thin and graceful as she moved about. Her English was quite good and her voice had the lilting, hypnotic quality of a person speaking a language not completely familiar to them. She smiled easily and genuinely cared for Dan. Marlin could see that the gruff old hunter cared for her as well. After a time, she excused herself and set about doing her kitchen chores. As she got up to leave, Dan said something to her in her native language. He was fluent in several languages and Marlin had no idea what he said but got the impression that it was something personal since she smiled and looked a little embarrassed. "What did you say to her?" he asked.

"Oh that," Dan answered. "Just a little game I play with her... nothing important."

Dan and Marlin sat for some time before he commented, "She's been with me for a long time Marley."

"I figured that," Marlin answered.

"It doesn't bother you? You don't think it's wrong... a white man with a black woman?"

Marlin asked him, "What does she think? Does she think it's wrong? Seems it could go both ways especially since out here you would be considered the oddity. I haven't been out here very long but it seems the rules from Europe or the States don't apply much out here... except to the people who brought the rules with them."

Dan didn't know how to respond and just sat there thinking. Marlin broke the silence, "I know you don't want to offend your clients and I understand that. I just don't want you to feel that you're going to offend me. This is your home... and as I understand it, it's her home too."

"I appreciate that," Dan responded and then changed the subject. "I have a client coming out here next month... wants to hunt a lion. I'd like to have you and Sironka take him on the hunt."

"Sure, we can do that. Any special reason?"

"No, not really... I just want to take a little time off."

"Anything I should know about this guy?" asked Marlin.

"I don't know him; never met him. I have no idea his level of experience... other than what he has told me in his letter, and we all know hunters and fisherman lie. His name is Percy Penfield. He's from New York... a very wealthy family in the newspaper business, but that's all I know about him. You know, I can't remember the last time I read a newspaper. I only see one or two a month out here. There's something else I'd like to talk to you about."

"Alright."

"Your father was one of the few men in my life I ever really felt close to... a man I could trust. He understood my life out here...

how I grew up here, my attachment to this land. When I heard he died, I cried like I had lost my brother. I can't ever go back to England... hell, go back... I've never even been there. England was my parent's home; never mine. I'm not like all these others who have come out here... they're English or Dutch or German... I'm African. There is something I'd like to ask you to do for me."

Marlin sat and listened to Bwana Dan and responded, "Go ahead."

"Now that you know about Mbali and me... I want to make sure if anything happens to me that she gets whatever I have. I don't have much by the standards of the European community out here but by African standards she could live long and well on what I have. I'd like you to see to it she gets what I have and it isn't stolen from her. The English or Germans or Dutch... whoever, will want the property to farm or continue the safari business so I can't leave it to her directly... they'll just figure out a way to cheat her. If I leave the property to you, they won't be able to cheat her."

"How do you propose I go about that?"

"See to it that my land is sold for a fair price and see that she gets the money... so she's taken care of. You're no fool Marley... nobody will be able to cheat you. I know at some point you'll be going back to Charleston, but you've got the connections to see that things get done proper even if you're not here."

"Well, I'm not planning to go back to Charleston real soon. You're not planning on dying real soon, are you?"

Bwana Dan laughed and responded, "No, I don't have any plans as of yet! When I slide into my grave it won't be until I'm completely worn out, used up and finished! I guess my hunt with Monty got me to thinking some. He was a good hunter and a good guy, but I just don't think he's going to get many more hunts. I don't think he's got many more years in him, though I do hope I'm wrong about that. I've beat the odds so far, but you've been out here long enough to know the dangers. Just living out here can be dangerous enough, but doing what we do for a living... dealing with some of the idiots we take on hunts... you've got to admit sometimes we press our luck. Sometimes a guy like Monty comes along... makes you stop and think."

Marlin didn't respond. He thought for a moment about Monty and Tina. He had learned something from each of them. For an instant he thought about telling Bwana Dan about Tina but then remembered what Bunny had told him and thought better of it.

They walked into the great room and Marlin changed the subject as he looked over the numerous books shelved on one of the walls. It was quite an extensive library and there was one section that caught Marlin's eye. There was one large section devoted to nothing but books and stories of the American West. "I noticed that you have quite a few western books," he commented.

"Yes indeed," Dan responded. "I've always been fascinated by cowboys and the western frontier... always thought I was born in the wrong time and on the wrong continent."

"That explains the Colt forty five, boots and cowboy hat," Marlin replied. "When I first came here Captain Mike told me to ask you about the zebra... but he said I should get to know you first before I asked."

A faraway look came over Dan's face for a moment and then he smiled. "I guess I know you well enough to tell you about that.

You're considered family... but you got to promise that you never repeat the story... especially to anyone like Bunny Allen! A story like this could stick to a person and people might think you're crazy... might not think of you as a serious hunter."

There was a pause before Dan started the story, "This all took place when I was about sixteen years old. My mother had died and my father had taken to the bottle. I retreated to my stories about the Wild West and cowboys. Out here our entertainment consists of reading and I've read every book on those shelves at least once and some more than once. I came up with the idea that I needed a horse like a real cowboy but there were no horses around here... but there are plenty of zebras. I thought that if I could domesticate a zebra, I could ride him like a horse. Can't you see how grand I'd look with my cowboy hat and boots on a striped horse?"

Marlin smiled at the thought and asked, "How did it work out?"

"Not so good. I caught a young zebra and kept him in a coral... he got to be pretty tame. At least I thought he was tame... he'd eat out of my hand and let me touch him. Then one day I thought I'd try to ride him... I even made a sort of saddle. My father was a little drunk sitting on the back porch watching all this when I got a couple of the boys to hold the zebra still so I could get on. The zebra wasn't at all happy about this and when they let go he started jumping and twisting... a real bucking bronc! I went up in the air one way and the zebra and my saddle went the other... never saw either one again. My father started laughing... he couldn't stop. Something in his mind just snapped. I don't really know what was going through his mind. Maybe the absurdity of his whole life became clear to him... he was castaway in Africa sent to bring Jesus to the savages... he failed at his mission... his wife dies of fever and now he is left with the vision of his idiot son trying to ride a zebra dressed up as a cowboy. It was about a week later when he died. I don't know if he laughed because it was funny or because it pointed out how insane it is to try to change Africa. I can laugh about it now... I bet I cut quite the dashing figure on my striped bronc!"

They stood there for a moment longer looking at the books. Dan had shared a story with Marlin that only a few people knew of. He was a more complicated man than what was on the surface and the story was personal. It was more than just a funny story of a boy and a zebra; there was an undertone of tragedy... it summed up the European colonization of Africa. Maybe there were just some places in the world that should remain untouched and wild.

Dan broke the silence, "I'll write up something in the next few days that will serve as my will and spell out everything so it will be all legal and such."

"Okay," Marlin responded, his thoughts about the bucking zebra interrupted. "That's a good idea... put it down in writing."

*Chapter 26*

# Life On The Savana

I t was about this time when Marlin began to go off into the savanna alone or with Sironka and stay away for days at a time. There were some favorite places he would go just to watch the animals and be part of their world. He and Sironka would often not speak for hours at a time, just walk and observe. At night they would build a fire and sit under the stars and sometimes talk about their lives or what they had witnessed.

After returning to the hunting lodge one day Bwana Dan asked him, "Where do you go when you go off alone?"

"Out there," Marlin answered. "No place special… just out there."

"I know how it is… a man needs to be alone sometimes. You can't be more alone than when you're out there… even if you're with another person. If you'd let me, next time you go, there's a place I'd like to show you… a place where you're father and I would go. I think you would like it."

About a week later, Bwana Dan and Marley set off into the savanna. They started at dawn and it was just before sundown they came upon a rise in the landscape that looked down on a large expanse. There was a small stream that opened into a wide area providing a large waterhole that was sure to attract game animals.

"This was your father's favorite spot. He would come here often and as he said 'watch life and death play out' in the savanna."

"It looks like a perfect hunting spot," replied Marlin.

"It is, for them," Dan replied as he pointed to the lions. "Your father and I made a vow to never hunt here. We wanted something out here to be completely untouched… at least by us. We better set up a camp before it gets too dark… and a good fire! Tomorrow we can watch an entire day play out in front of us."

They built a campfire and cooked some dinner. After dinner, Dan broke out a bottle of whisky, poured them each a drink, filled his pipe with tobacco and lit up. It wasn't long before they could hear the roar of lions and other animal sounds in the night.

"From the sound of that it seems they made a kill," stated Marlin.

"That's good for us," replied Dan. "They'll feast all night and won't be sniffing around here thinking about eating us! It's good to have a big fire just the same."

Dan went on to relate a lion story. "Many years ago there was a rouge lion... a big male, terrorizing one of the villages around here. The natives were all very afraid since he had killed and eaten four people. Apparently he had developed a taste for humans rather than livestock... and probably found they were easier to catch. The villagers placed fires around where the livestock was to keep the lion away but they had to man the fires with people to keep them burning. In the morning two more men were missing and when they found the remains there was no doubt the lion had killed them."

"The fire didn't keep him away?" asked Marlin.

"That's what the natives thought. Now they believed it was a sort of spirit lion, unafraid of fire... a lion they couldn't kill, so they contacted me. I checked into it and figured the lion waited until the flames went down and was just creeping closer, waiting in the shadows. When a native got up and went to get some wood for the fire... or stepped into the shadows to take a leak, guess who was waiting for him."

"So you killed him?"

"Yes... I hunted him down and killed him. A rouge lion is the deadliest because they will always charge. They're not afraid of humans... they eat humans and know how weak we are... showing a lion a gun doesn't scare them... they don't know what a gun is. I've got to say, that was about the most scared I've ever been on a hunt."

"You were scared? I can't believe that."

"I'm human Marley... I get scared sometimes. Don't you?" Dan asked as he puffed on his pipe.

"Sure, but I'm pretty new to this. You've been out here for years."

"Doesn't matter," Dan went on. "Man is the only animal that can reason... think his way out of a problem... provided fear doesn't over-ride his ability to think. When you watch a lion chase a gazelle they are both reacting. The lion chases to relieve his hunger and the gazelle runs out of fear... neither is doing any reasoning, they are both just reacting. The lion has learned over time the best method to catch the gazelle and the gazelle has learned the best method to avoid getting caught. One will win and one will lose... it just takes one mistake by one of them. "

"Think about when you hunt," he went on. "When you approach a dangerous animal, you think about how it might play out... is the gun loaded... when you can make the shot... where to move for protection... wind direction... how to get the advantage. You prepare to avoid panic."

"Is that what keeps you from being afraid?" questioned Marlin.

"Fear is a good thing. Keeps us from doing stupid things or at least it should. If you're about to do something dangerous... something you've chosen to do... if you're not a little fearful, then you're just a fool. It's when you panic and can't think, that's when you're doomed."

"Sironka says the fire keeps the demons and spirits away," Marlin stated. "And to never walk in the night shadows."

"Well, I don't know about spirits and such but I know the lions will watch us from a distance. They won't come near the fire but like Sironka says, if you walk into the shadows you're fair game. Other animals, not so much, but lions will wait and watch."

The next morning the two men watched from their vantage point as life played out in Africa. The various grazing animals moved about and attempted to stay alert to any of the meat eaters ready to make them a meal. Marlin watched and commented, "I wonder what they think about."

Bwana Dan responded, "I don't believe they think... at least not like men think. From a purely religious point of view, the animals are here to live out their intended purpose and to be ruled over by man... if you believe that sort of thing."

"And you don't believe that?"

"Only to a point," Dan continued. "They are here to maintain life, that is to say, to be eaten by other animals. Little fish get eaten by bigger fish and so on. Gazelles get eaten by lions and when the lion gets old and dies the vultures get them... but they don't think and reason, they react to their instincts."

"What about when they hunt?" Marlin countered. "They work as a team. That must take some thinking."

"I didn't say they were stupid. Over the years they have learned what is successful. Those that didn't learn died off... you know, the Darwin thing. They can learn that a man is an easy meal but I believe the animals can only live in the moment... they don't think past the immediate situation. The lion comes, the gazelle runs, its win or lose... it's not personal, it's just life. You can learn a lot from the male lion. His life is spent eating, sleeping, fighting off rivals and humping the females. As long as he can keep his rivals away his life goes on that way... until he is beaten or killed... for most of the animals here, it's the same story... just life on the savanna."

"And the ruled over by man part of this?" Marlin questioned. "How do you work that out?"

"That's the most interesting part. Man is the most dangerous animal because he does think. He plots and schemes... reasons and rationalizes, to get what he wants."

"You don't have a very high regard for mankind do you?" Marlin laughed.

"I guess not," Dan answered. "But we do devour our own... not from the cannibal view but just the basic inhumanity we engage in. The animals are honest about it. The gazelle knows the lion will eat him if he gets a chance... no illusions, no treachery, just reality.

"I don't share your level of distrust. I'm not naive, I know there are untrustworthy people out there but I believe most people, given the chance, will do the right thing."

Bwana Dan smiled and then replied, "You must get that from your father. He believed that way too. He provided a bit of balance to my darker view of life. When I go to that dark place I often think about him and what he would say. When we would come here we would often have these types of discussions... that was why I wanted to bring you out here to show you this place. People like me need a Robert Colby to give us perspective... and people like you need people like me to remind you that rouge lions are out there... and the only way to deal with a rouge lion is to face it and kill it."

## Chapter 27

# Percy Penfield

**M**arlin was sitting on the porch as the sun was beginning to dip lower in the sky when the roadster pulled into the compound. Marlin got his first look at Percy Penfield at that moment. He was seated in the back seat smoking a cigarette held in a long cigarette holder, his driver seated in front of him. He looked to be about thirty five had an aloof, snobbish look about him. When the car stopped, the driver jumped quickly from his seat and rushed to open the door for his passenger. Penfield stepped out of the car and immediately barked orders at his driver, "Get my luggage inside and be damn careful with those rifles."

Marlin stood up as Percy Penfield approached the stairs to the lodge. "Good evening, you must be Mister Penfield, I'm Marlin Colby," he stated as he extended his hand.

"Yes, I'm Percy Penfield, pleased to meet you. Mister Crowley is expecting me, is he about?" he asked refusing to take Marlin's hand.

"Yes, he's inside."

"Good. Are you a guest or a hunter?" Penfield inquired.

"I work here for Mister Crowley..."

"Fine," Penfield interrupted in a curt tone. "See to it that my driver gets my luggage and rifles to my room without damaging anything. He's all that I could find out here and he's truly an idiot. The only reason I hired him was he spoke English well enough so I could tell him what to do."

With his instructions given he quickly entered the lodge to find Bwana Dan. Marlin's first encounter with Percy Penfield didn't impress him, but he had seen enough rich, snobbish hunters to not really care either way. He went off to help the driver, a small Hindu man, who was struggling with the luggage cases.

"Let me help you with that."

"Thank you Sahib... there are many bags!" he replied gratefully.

"Take a few bags... I'll take the gun cases... come back for the rest."

"Be oh so careful Sahib... my Master yells at me whenever I touch them!"

"I'll be careful, come with me."

With the luggage and rifles put away, Marlin went about his business. An hour or so went by before he entered the great room and bar. Penfield was standing at the bar with Dan. He had changed clothes and was wearing dark grey slacks, white shirt and dark blue dinner jacket… and still smoking a cigarette with the long holder. As he entered, Dan saw him and motioned him over, "Marlin, come over here. Let me introduce you to Percy Penfield."

"We've met," Marlin replied coolly. "Your luggage and rifles are in your room as you requested. Your driver will be in the room next to you so you'll be able to yell for him when you need him."

Marlin went behind the bar to pour himself a drink, not caring to engage Penfield in anything but polite conversation. As the son of a very wealthy man, he remembered his father always telling him that money didn't give you the right to be an asshole, although he didn't put it in those exact words because he was a young boy at the time. His first impression of Percy Penfield was that he was an asshole.

Bwana Dan, as always, was the perfect host, seeing to it that his guest had a drink and assuring him that dinner would be served shortly. "Percy has come out here to hunt a lion," Dan announced. "You'll find him a grand trophy won't you Marley!"

With that announcement Penfield's expression changed. He had the look of a man who had just been cheated out of something and he wasn't going to stand for it. "I was under the impression that you were going to lead my hunt Mister Crowley," he stated in a very formal tone.

"No, I'm going to have Marley and another guide take you."

"I am paying a great deal of money for this hunt. I want an experienced guide. This young man can't be more than twenty five years old!"

Dan was always polite when dealing with clients but sometimes he just couldn't help his contempt from sneaking through. "Have you ever shot a lion Mister Penfield?"

"No, of course not, that's why I'm here!"

"Marlin has shot many... including several dangerous rouge animals... man eaters. That's why he's taking you. I know my business Mister Penfield. Marley will get you on a lion... all you will have to do is shoot it. If you miss, it's his job to see that the lion doesn't kill you."

The tension was eased with the announcement that dinner was served. Penfield made some attempt at smoothing over his condescending remarks during dinner. He was more than pleased to talk about himself and all that he had done. Dan became charming once again and Marlin remained polite. It was soon learned that Percy Penfield's hunting experience was limited. He had shot deer, elk and bear in North America... although it was a black bear, not a grizzly. He had been mountain lion hunting as well, but in that type of hunt dogs were used to tree the cat and the hunter shot it out of the tree. Hunting an African lion was going to be much more dangerous.

It seems that his father had sent him off to go on these adventures and then write about his exploits. He was employed by the newspaper but was not involved in its operation... simply a guest writer at his father's discretion. After college, Penfield went to work for his father and then his father sent him off on this assignment.

"So how many articles do you send into the paper," Dan asked.

"Oh, I only send in a few a year."

"So you've been traveling the world hunting and writing. Sounds like a great lifestyle."

"After this Africa trip I'd like to stay in the States for some time. We'll see... my father tells me that he'd like some articles on big game fishing."

After Penfield went off to bed, Dan asked Marlin to join him in the bar. "Marley," he began. "You need to be careful of this guy. He could be a real problem."

Marlin listened as Dan went on, "His father has sent him away for a reason... probably paying him a remittance just to stay away! Probably because he's an asshole!"

Marlin smiled as Dan continued, "I'm serious, I've seen this type of guy out here before... more money than sense. Cocky, arrogant and no real hunting experience... at least not with something like a lion. If he'd shot a grizzly, then I might be impressed. Be careful. This is the type of guy that can get you killed!"

*Chapter 28*

# Lion Hunt

**M**arlin walked out of his bungalow and immediately saw that Percy Penfield was in a heated argument with his Hindu servant. The body language of the servant was apparent; his arms crossed in front of him and his head shaking side to side. As he approached he could hear the conversation and realized what was going on.

"No... no, I will not do it," the servant kept saying while continuing to shake his head. "You said nothing of this... I will not be eaten by a lion!"

"I hired you! You will do as I say!" Penfield insisted.

The conversation was at a standstill with neither side giving in. They were so involved in the quarrel they didn't notice Marlin. "Good morning gentleman… it's a good day for a lion hunt."

"No, it is not a good day! It is a bad day… a very bad day! I will not hunt a lion!" the servant exclaimed as he stomped away.

"Damn idiot! What am I paying you for? Come back here this instant!" Penfield shouted at the retreating Hindu.

Marlin looked over the impeccably dressed Percy Penfield. His clothes were starched and pressed and he had what appeared to be a new scoped rifle slung over his shoulder. "It appears your man servant has no interest in lion hunting," Marlin commented with a hint of a smile.

"I want him to be my gun bearer… carry my rifle on the hunt."

"Yes, about your rifle. Looks like a new Mauser Africa Model. I would guess a 9.3 X 62… would you like to take a couple of practice shots and make sure it's alright."

"No," Penfield snapped. "I had the gunsmith sight it in already. It's perfect."

"The gunsmith?" Marlin questioned. "Not you?"

"I've been assured that it is perfectly sighted for two hundred yards."

Marlin was beginning to see what Bwana Dan was talking about. "Everybody's eyes are different. Yours are different than the gunsmith… scope relief and such. Have you fired the gun?"

"Yes, I've fired the damn gun! That's not the problem. Who's going to carry it for me? That's the problem!"

At that point, Sironka approached. He was dressed in his red native attire and carrying his spear. He said nothing, just stood silently a few feet away looking Percy Penfield over.

"I see your bearer has arrived," Penfield noted.

"Sironka is not my bearer. He is a Massai warrior and will be a guide."

"Well, then he can leave the spear behind and carry my rifle."

Marlin was beginning to get annoyed, "The Massai hunt lions with a spear. He will not be leaving it behind or carrying your rifle. I carry my own rifle... I suggest you do the same, things can happen quickly out here, but if you would like I'll get one of the other boys to act as bearer for you." With that, Marlin called over a small boy and gave him some instructions in Swahili. He ran off and in a few minutes two native bearers arrived.

"Now, about that rifle..." Marlin started before Penfield cut him off.

"What about my rifle. What's wrong with it?"

"Lion hunting is a close up game. We're going to stalk a lion and move in close for the kill... probably as close as thirty yards. A scope would be fine for a long range shot at a gazelle. You might want to pull that scope off and use your iron sights. With the heavy bullet your using at that close range you'll be firing high... you'd have to adjust your aim point... possibly at a charging lion."

"My rifle will be fine... I'll just aim lower. How far do we have to walk to find a lion?"

"Not far I expect... we're in the heart of lion country. We'll move towards a watering hole I know of. We usually find lions nearby. This first time out, we'll try to locate the lions and do some scouting… see if we can find you a trophy. We'll find one and study him a bit, then set about stalking and hunting him tomorrow… provided we find a good one today."

Marlin had a bearer for Penfield and a couple of others to carry some water and a bit of food. Sironka walked next to Marlin and Percy Penfield followed about twenty feet behind just strolling along. Unlike Monty who was curious about animals and tracking, he said nothing, just followed along. Occasionally, Sironka and Marlin would stop and point out something to each other but Penfield showed no particular interest. It was as if he were being taken on a walking tour of Africa and at some point he would just shoot a lion as part of the tour. As they got close to the waterhole, Sironka said something to Marlin in his native tongue that was uncomplimentary about Penfield and Marlin laughed.

Penfield, suspecting that he was the topic of conversation immediately wanted to know what was said, "What did he say? Was he talking about me?"

"Oh, no," Marlin explained. "Just a little inside joke… nothing about you."

"Well, it's damn rude. He should speak English, not that native gibberish."

They located some lions napping not too far from the waterhole. The bearer gave Penfield his rifle and Marlin, Sironka and Penfield started to move closer to get a better look. Marlin whispered to Penfield, "We're going to move off to their flank. There's a male over there that I want to get a look at. The wind direction is good and there's plenty of cover… keep in mind cover for us is also cover for them. There may be something between us and that male we haven't seen."

They moved closer. Marlin was in the middle, Penfield was to the right and Sironka was on his left. "The big male should be just over there," Marlin pointed. "We'll get a look at him and see if he's a good one."

Marlin turned his head to get a visual on Sironka who was crouched low behind a bush. It was in that instant the gun blast was heard. Penfield had fired. "I got him! I got him!" he screamed.

"What the hell did you do?" Marlin shouted.

"I shot him. He was right there… I saw him right there, so I fired!"

Sironka had run over as Marlin grabbed Penfield and shouted, "Back out! Move back! Don't let him get on our flank!" They started to move back as they heard the lion let out a fierce roar from deep in the brush.

They moved back to a position of relative safety and got their bearings. Sironka was the first to speak, "Lion is mad. Only hurt. He will not die soon."

The lion was only wounded as Penfield's shot had been high hitting him in the left flank doing little damage. He fired quickly and didn't strike the lion in any vital area. While he couldn't move as quickly as before, the lion would still be hard to hit on the move. He was wounded, mad and felt cornered. He was now hunting the hunters.

"We'll move towards him. The sound came from over there," Marlin directed. "I'll take a point position… Penfield, you'll be on my right about five yards behind me… Sironka on my left at the same distance. Penfield, reload the round you fired. Be ready to shoot fast, he'll probably charge us."

Penfield stood frozen. He heard the instructions but was failing to respond. Marlin knew that they had to move quickly. The lion knew where they were so they were going to have to force him to move in order to get a shot. They would have to stay close and in a triangle formation so they could best protect each other.

Marlin was quickly losing patience with Penfield, "For God's sake, get yourself together! Load the damn gun! You wanted to hunt a lion... you were too far away and made a bad shot so now you have to finish it!"

Penfield came out of his daze and with unsteady hands loaded his gun. "Okay... I'm ready," he responded, his voice shaking a bit.

They moved forward into the waist high grass. There were several downed trees and rocks amongst the grass offering plenty of hiding places. Marlin kept his rifle on his shoulder in a low ready position so he would be able to make a fast shot. Penfield at first just carried his rifle low and off his shoulder until he saw what Marlin was doing. At that point he moved his rifle into the same position. He was so nervous that sweat was getting into his eyes and he was having difficulty seeing. He felt like he was going to throw up. Sironka held his spear low and pointed straight in front of him at waist high.

There was a low deep growl that came from the right flank and then a quick movement. Marlin shouted, "Penfield! On your right! There he is! Shoot!" Penfield turned and faced the lion. He had a clear shot but he froze with fear for an instant, then turned to run, took two steps, tripped and fell to the ground in a fetal position. The lion saw him go down and was almost on him. Sironka was the closest to him and also turned to face the lion. The lion leaped over Penfield's body when he saw the standing Massai warrior. Sironka was not able to get his spear in position quickly enough to get a fatal wound as the lion sprung. The spear penetrated the lion's body and the weight of the beast carried him towards Sironka. His massive claws slashed across Sironka's face and neck, ripping through his jugular vein and killing him almost instantly. Marlin had to spin completely around to get his gun on the lion that now had an additional wound inflicted by Sironka before he was killed. Before he could take aim, the lion had vanished like a ghost into the tall grass.

The lion was now moving more slowly. The spear had caused enough damage and there was now a blood trail to follow. Marlin quickly followed the trail, leaving the useless Penfield behind and found the lion crouched and growling as he approached. The animal was severely wounded, bleeding but not close to death and still very dangerous. There was a moment where they both just stared at each other before the big cat dug in his back feet preparing to make his final charge. The lion stared at Marlin, his large yellow eyes had a look of rage... and not a bit of fear. Marlin set his feet, took aim and fired hitting the lion directly in the center of his forehead as he began his charge. The animal went down stopping just a few feet from Marlin. In a fit of anger and frustration, Marlin fired two more shots into the lions head at close range.

He stood there a few moments just looking at the lion, his mind catching up on all that took place in a matter of just a few seconds, before he realized Percy Penfield was approaching. As he walked up Penfield yelled, "My trophy lion! You destroyed my lion! Look at his head… you destroyed it!"

At that point Marlin exploded with rage. He turned to Penfield and punched him directly in the center on his face. Penfield reeled backwards and Marlin punched him in the face again, this time knocking him to the ground, unconscious. He took Penfield's rifle and smashed it over a rock. He then called out to some native bearers hiding off in the distance and returned to where the lifeless Sironka lay.

He was kneeling over his friend's body when the bearers came on scene. Sironka's lifeless eyes stared blankly up into the sky. He tenderly took his hand and closed Sironka's eyes then directed the bearers to make a stretcher and to carry Sironka to his homestead so his family could follow proper burial tradition. Penfield had regained consciousness and walked up on the scene. His face was bleeding, he was unsteady and he was angry, "Who do you think you are? You can't treat me this way…"

"Shut up!" Marlin shouted back at him. Then he grabbed him and pushed him over to where Sironka lay dead. "Look at him!" he ordered. "You're cowardice caused this. A brave man died because you failed to act. He saved your miserable ass and all you're worried about is *your trophy*…"

Penfield retorted in an arrogant tone, "What's so important? He just a…"

Marlin grabbed him by the throat stopping him mid-sentence as the bearers looked on in fear, never having seen Bwana Marley so angry or upset. He pointed his rifle directly between Penfield's eyes, "Don't say it! I'm warning you. I'm just about ready to leave you out here to fend for yourself! That man lying there was a warrior... a great warrior... a great hunter and my friend. Your best bet right now is to shut up and say nothing or so help me I'll kill you myself and leave you for the hyenas!"

*Chapter 29*

# Letter From Home

Three weeks had passed since the Percy Penfield incident. Before he left he made a variety of threats to publish an article in his father's newspaper about how badly he was treated on his hunt and the incompetence of all involved... with the exception of himself, of course. Bwana Dan pointed out to him that his father only had one newspaper and that not only was he capable of writing an article himself, but was more than sure that his father's competitors would be interested in the cowardly exploits of a son paid to stay away from home. Dan also pointed out to Penfield that while Africa was a big place, the hunting guide community was small and the word was already out about him. He strongly suggested that he leave Africa and never come back.

It was about that time that Marlin got a letter from his sister Alice.

> *Dear Marley,*
>
> *I'm writing to let you know that mother has been ill. While her health has not been good recently, the doctor tells us this is much more serious. You've been gone for so long. It's been almost five years. Can you please come home? Mother may not have a great deal of time left. It may be your last chance to see her. She talks of you often and misses you. Nothing has changed with George. He is still about and trying to force his will on mother. If it wasn't for Sean, I'm sure he would try to do something underhanded.*
>
> *I have been seeing a great deal of Sean and he has asked me to marry him. I am very much in love with him and said "yes". I know you asked him to keep where you are and what you're doing a secret but after my constant badgering he finally gave in and told me of your exploits. Please don't be angry with him. He is truly a good and loyal friend. I hope you will give your blessing to our marriage.*
>
> *Please come home Marley.*
>
> *All my love,*
>
> *Alice*

Marlin read the letter and set it down. Five years... has it been that long. Two years on the *Shamrock Isle* and over three years in

Africa… it didn't seem possible. He sat there for a long while just thinking. It had been a long time since he thought about Charleston and all that had happened. It seemed like such a long time ago now. Black Johnny and the Spaniard had been right… life did go on. It seemed he originally left home just to run away from all that happened. Then it became somewhat of a journey to learn more about his father, but in the process he learned about himself.

He would have to go back. He knew he had no choice in that and he knew it all along. Sironka knew it too… Marlin's lion didn't live in Africa. Leaving Africa would be difficult. He liked it there. He liked the people, the animals, the adventure, the wildness of the place. Returning to Charleston would be difficult… facing the old demons again, but perhaps life has gone on there as well and he was forgotten. He would go back, to see his mother and sister, he would face his demons, but only to visit, he would not plan to stay. He would return to Africa.

It was over dinner when he broke the news to Dan and Mbali. "Dan, I got a letter from Charleston today… from my sister. My mother is very ill… it doesn't look good."

"Well, I expect you'll be heading home soon."

"I don't think I have much of a choice," Marlin replied.

"We always have a choice, but you'll do the right thing, just like your father would. It's what he would expect and what I would expect. But you'll be back because Africa is a part of you now. In the short time you've been here you've made a name for yourself as a great hunter but more importantly, the people here trust you. I'll go with you to the city when you decide it's time… I have the legal paperwork we spoke of to drop off with an attorney."

"How's the day after tomorrow?" Marlin asked. "I don't have a lot of gear to pack up but there's something I'd like to do tomorrow."

"That's fine. I'll make sure the truck is ready."

Mbali started to tear up and excused herself from the table. "No tears woman," Dan ordered. "He'll only be gone a short while. He'll be back."

The next day Marlin took his rifle and set off early in the morning to go to Sironka's homestead. He didn't really know why. Tradition would dictate there would be no grave but he wanted to go there just the same. When he arrived there was great fanfare and excitement. Apparently, unbeknownst to him, Sironka had talked him up as a great hunter and other tribe members who had been in contact with him had more than embellished the tales. The fact that he came to the homestead to pay his respects and honor his friend was well received.

While he was there he came to find that Sironka was actually placed in a grave because over the years as a warrior and hunter he had become a wealthy influential member of the tribe. Marlin was taken to the gravesite and humbly knelt at his friend's grave. This type of reverence towards a member of their tribe by a white hunter had never been witnessed before and the tribe became jubilant, breaking into dancing and chanting. Before leaving, Marlin met Sironka's wife and children. His oldest son began speaking but Marlin only understood part of what he was saying. He presented Marlin with his father's spear and indicated that Marlin was his father's white brother. Marlin took off his hunting knife and presented it to Sironka's oldest son and told him to keep it always as a sign of Marlin's love and respect for his father.

Just before sunrise the next day Marlin said good bye to Mbali and the tears welled up in her dark eyes. "No need to cry... I'll be coming back," he told her as he gave her a hug.

"Off we go then," Dan commented as he put Marlin's gear in the truck. "Long trip to the city... won't get there unless we get started. Don't mind her now, she'll be fine. She thinks of you as her son being sent out into the world... afraid she might not see you again. I'll explain it to her and make it right."

It was a long trip to the city. Dan and Marlin spoke of many things, mostly hunting and Africa. At one point Dan got serious, "Captain Mike told me about all that happened back in Charleston... I never mentioned it before now... I figured if you wanted to say something... I didn't want to stick my nose in where maybe it shouldn't be..."

"It's okay," Marlin said. "Captain Mike, Black Johnny, the Spaniard, you... none of you ever passed judgment... it all seems like it happened a lifetime ago."

"When you're young, it is a lifetime ago. Things happen to people... just part of life. It's a matter of how you face up to it that counts."

"Like not running away from it," Marlin said in a soft tone.

"I don't see it that way," Dan reflected. "Sometimes you have to be prepared to face up to things... you need some time to work things through. In your case you're going back. Your mother being ill is a big part of it, but you know you'll have to face everything else as well. You could have rationalized a reason not to go back, but that's not who you are. Your path took you to sea and then to Africa but in the end you have to make your way back to Charleston... and you're not the same person you were when you left."

"What do you think my father would do? What if I fail?"

"I think you know exactly what he would do. You father was a gentleman. He was gracious and considerate... but he was also an Irishman, so he wasn't a man to cross! I never saw him start a fight but there were plenty of times when I saw him end one! You're his son and the similarities are remarkable. When the time comes, you'll do what you need to do."

Dan continued, "Every man has doubts. Your father had doubts and concerns when he started his shipping business. I remember him saying, 'the surest way to fail is to never try'... it was true then and it's true now."

Marlin smiled and commented, "I appreciate the confidence but how can you be so sure?"

"Because when you had to shoot a hyena on a dead run, you didn't think about it, you did it."

"It's not just about me anymore," Marlin reflected. "My mother is dying and things have to be set right for her as well. What do you think happens to you when you die?"

"Are you asking me if I believe in God?"

"I don't know... I was young when I lost my father and I was scared more than anything. When Mary died I was mad... I was angry... I felt a pain like I have never experienced. Now I will lose my mother and I know how much she believes... does it matter?"

"I don't know if it matters at all. My parents were religious people but I'm really not. It seems we believe what we are taught to believe when we're children... if the two people you rely on most… the two people who raise you tell you something, it must be true. It must give a certain level of comfort believing there is something waiting beyond our lives here."

"But what do you believe?" Marlin pressed.

"I don't believe there is anything waiting after death," Dan replied bluntly. "It would be nice to actually know if there was something beyond… it would be nice to get a post card from the great beyond to let a person know how great heaven is… provided they went that way! Your father was a believer, as well as your mother and I hope they're right."

"Why do you think all these different religions believe there is something after death? Even the natives here in Africa believe in something after death?" Marlin questioned.

"Marley, there's nothing wrong with belief in something beyond, but you can't let the certainty of death cripple you in life. When your father died it would be natural to be afraid. A father, especially one like yours, can seem larger than life… strong, invincible. It's hard to imagine them ever dying and it comes as a shock. Your mother has lived a long and productive life. Providing comfort and care… spending those precious last days is important, but you know it's coming and it doesn't seem as unfair. The death of Mary on the other hand will always leave a deeper scar. When the person is young and you are in love with them, the unfairness of it all… the anger, the pain is greater. I can only relate it to losing a fellow soldier in combat… friends who are like your brother. When they lose their lives at such a young age and you are a young person yourself… it's always, 'Why them? Not me? What could I have done different?' If you survive, you owe the person who didn't a good life… a life they would have been proud you lived. I'm not saying you ever forget. I'm saying that you put it behind you and move forward. No man goes to the grave free of regrets… there will always be a few, but most of the time you have no control over the circumstances."

When they finally arrived in the city it was several hours after sunset. The next morning they went to the lawyer's office and Dan had the paperwork completed. The terms were that in the event of his death, his property would be left to Marlin. Marlin, in turn, would liquidate the holdings and see that Mbali was taken care of. After the visit to the lawyer, Marlin went to the shipyard to check and see if the *Shamrock Isle* might be due in port. He found the ship was expected to dock in about a week if the weather held. Dan and Marlin got accommodations at a hotel for the night and Dan left to head back the next day.

It was about a week later when the *Shamrock Isle* docked. Marlin was at the dock when the gangplank was lowered. He walked up the gangplank and yelled, "Permission to come aboard?"

The sailors were busy and didn't notice who it was right away. It was Black Johnny who saw him first, "Hey… it's Marley! Spaniard… Captain Mike… it's Marley!"

Captain Mike came out of the wheel house with a broad smile on his face then shouted, "I'm glad ta see you're still alive. I expected ta hear ya been ate up by some wild beast… or them cannibals! Come aboard!"

It was a grand reunion with Captain Mike and the crew.

*Chapter 30*

# Sam Wiggins

Sam Wiggins opened his eyes and tried to focus. Everything around him looked white. He tried to move and found that he couldn't... then fear set in and he started to yell. He felt a hand on his forehead and realized a woman was looking at him. "Quiet down. You're okay. Don't struggle," she said as she applied a cool, wet cloth to his head.

"Who are you? Where am I?" Sam demanded.

"You're at the County Hospital. You're very sick. Calm down and I'll get the doctor."

Sam lay there and then realized he was strapped to the bed. He had found himself in this spot before when he was suffering from the DT's. As he started to regain his senses he relaxed a bit, thinking he had figured out what had happened. A doctor approached followed by the nurse.

"Undo the retention straps nurse... I don't think we'll need them for the time being."

"Yes doctor," she replied as she started to release the straps.

The doctor immediately listened to Sam's heart with his stethoscope before introducing himself. "I'm Doctor Adams," he stated. "But we don't know who you are. What's your name?"

"Sam... Sam... Wiggins," he replied having trouble for an instant remembering his last name. "What happened? How did I get here?"

"A couple of fisherman found you down by the river. They thought you were dead and called the police. When the officer determined you were still alive you were brought here. Do you remember anything? How you got to the river?"

Sam tried to remember but was still confused, "I don't remember nothin'. Can I go home now?"

"Do you have anyone who can care for you?"

"I can take care of myself okay," Sam responded in a weak but indignant tone.

"I don't think you'll be ready to go home for a while," Doctor Adams replied in a soft voice. "You're going to need a great deal of rest."

"No. I'm goin' home," Sam stated, and then tried to get up.

He couldn't move. He was in such a weakened state that he could barely raise his head off his pillow. "What's wrong? What's wrong with me? I can't move."

"When you arrived here you were barely alive. In fact, I'm surprised that you are still with us. You started to have some convulsions so we had to restrain you. I didn't think you would make it through the night. You've been sick for some time, haven't you? And there has been a great deal of pain and you've lost a great deal of weight... right?"

"I've been feelin' poorly for a while... I don't rightly know how long. I take some moonshine now and again if I get to hurtin'."

"I don't know how to say this, other than to just tell you straight," the doctor began. "I'm sorry... everything I have seen points to you having cancer and I believe you have a very short time to live."

"Can't you do something? Can't you operate?" Sam pleaded.

"I'm sorry. There's nothing we can do for you. Your condition is inoperable. Do you have any family we can contact?"

Sam wanted to scream. He wanted to get out of the bed and punch the doctor in the face. He tried to move and was just too weak. All he could say was, "I got no kin. How much time do I got?"

"Anywhere between six hours and six days. We'll make you as comfortable as we can," the doctor replied before rising from the bedside. "I'll check in on you a little later."

Sam Wiggins was left to lie in his bed. He started to weep as the realization of his death set in. There would be no quick, painless death for Sam. No gentle passing in his sleep. He would have to lie in bed waiting for the grim reaper to come, afraid to close his eyes, fearing they would never reopen. At first he refused to believe his situation... then he felt the pain and knew his body was dying from the inside out. He prayed for a miracle... divine intervention.

A few hours passed before Doctor Adams returned and announced, "I'm going to give you a shot for the pain."

"Wait Doc. Will it put me to sleep? I can't go to sleep yet! I need to talk to a priest. Can you find one for me? I can't close my eyes yet!"

Doctor Adams honored Sam's request and held off on the shot. He called Father Bernard, a priest who visited patients at the hospital or in jail on a regular basis. When Father Bernard arrived, he gave him what little background he had on Sam Wiggins, then took him to Sam. Father Bernard was a soft spoken, smallish, slight built man in his late sixties with thinning grey hair and dark blue eyes. He was semi-retired in terms of his Church duties but always made himself available to anyone in need. After introducing him to Sam, Doctor Adams left them alone.

Father Bernard started to prepare to administer the last rites to Sam, but Sam stopped him. "No need for all that Father... you should know, I'm not Catholic. In fact, up until about an hour ago I never gave any thought to any kind of religion... but now, I'm kinda in a fix."

"What can I do for you?" Father Bernard asked.

"I don't wanna die," Sam pleaded. "I thought maybe if I talked to you... did one of those confessions... admit to all the wrong I done... maybe you could help me out..."

Father Bernard had heard the confessions of many men condemned to death as well as of those with terminal medical conditions. He had heard many men try to make a deal to get out of what was inevitable. He knew he was dealing with a scared and desperate man.

"Sam, I can help you to pass from this world and into the next with a heart unburdened by guilt or shame... only God has the power to decide when you will pass... and there is a time for each of us."

After a bit more explanation, Sam Wiggins finally accepted what he knew all along, that no one could bargain their way out of death. He cried for a while before regaining his composure. "So if I talk to you... tell you all the bad stuff I done... my heart will be what you said... unburdened..."

"Yes, but you also have to pledge not to do the same things again and God will forgive you," the priest explained.

"Well, it don't seem too likely I'll be gettin' the chance to do much more sinnin'," Sam replied in a brief moment of levity.

After that Sam Wiggins proceeded to confess to an entire life filled with wrong doing. Most of his activities were mundane but every now and then there would be a depraved act that was shocking even to a priest who had heard most everything. Finally Sam got to the story of the car crash and how he was responsible for the death of Mary Luchetti and setting up Marlin to take the blame. He admitted the death of the young girl had haunted him and he had seen her face in his nightmares. He was getting tired and weak towards the end of his confession when he asked, "Father, is there anything I can do to make my life right?"

"Your confession was told to me in confidence. You have left that young man with a horrible burden he must carry through his entire life... the belief that he was responsible for a young girl's death. I cannot act on what you've told me without your permission."

Sam Wiggins looked at Father Bernard and begged, "Promise me you will make it right. I haven't done much right in my whole life… I'm sorry for what I done. Please find him… let him know I'm sorry for what I done. Please see if you can't make at least that one thing right."

"I'll find him and make it as right as I can," he promised.

"Thanks. I guess I do feel better 'bout dying now… even though I still don't wanna. Could you tell the Doc I could use that shot now… the pain is getting' real bad… I'd like to close my eyes an' get some sleep."

*Chapter 31*

# Home Coming

Marlin stood on the deck as the *Emerald Isle* docked in Charleston. The voyage had been a reunion with his old shipmates and a chance to think over all that had taken place in the last five years. He had a feeling of excitement as he thought about seeing his mother and sister as well as a reluctance to leave the security of the ship. He stayed aboard and helped with the normal duties associated with docking. Finally when there was no more work Captain Mike spoke, "I guess you'll be headin' home now... seein' yer mother an' sister."

"Yeah, I guess I'll be getting my stuff and heading home," he replied in a somewhat reluctant tone.

"Tell yer mother I'll be comin' by ta see her in a couple of days. Ya know Marley, ya ain't the same man ya was when ya signed on board. Ya was a scared kid back then… you're a grown man now. Ya been ta sea… ya been ta Africa. Whatever comes yer way, ya can handle it."

Marlin knew what Captain Mike was referring to and wasn't as confident as he was. He took a long walk through Charleston on his way home. Some things had changed but most things had remained the same. Eventually he found himself standing in front of his home and realized walking through that door would bring him back to where his journey had started… along with the reasons why. He also knew there was no going back so he walked up on the porch and knocked on the door.

When the door opened, there stood Calvin who looked at the young man at the door without recognizing him. "Hello Calvin," Marlin began. "I've come home."

The old man looked at him more closely and tears started to well up in his eyes, "Master Marley… it really is you! Come in! Come in!" Then he started shouting, "Miss Sally… Miss Sally… come quick! You brother is home! Your mother will be so happy!"

Marlin entered the house and set his sea bag on the floor. It looked the same; nothing was out of place or changed from when he left. His sister, Sally, entered the room and jumped into his arms. She was no longer the young girl he knew when he left, she was now a young woman.

"Oh Marley," she exclaimed. "You've finally come home! We've missed you so much! And just look at you! You're all grown up!"

"Seems you've done some growing up, too," Marlin replied. "And what's this I hear about you getting married! You're much too young to get married!"

"I am not!" she retorted. "Isn't it wonderful… Sean and I will marry in the Spring."

"Yes, it's wonderful. Sean is a fine man. I wish you both every happiness. Where's mother? How's she doing?"

"She's out on the back porch, sitting in the sun. She's been about the same… very tired but very much in touch with all that goes on. Your being here will give her a big boost. Come, I'll take you to her."

On their way to the back of the house, Marlin asked, "And what of Reilly? Bring me up to date on him."

Sally stopped mid stride, "Marley… please say nothing of him to mother. She is so ashamed. He comes in and out at will but normally says out at night. It's well known that he has been seeing another woman. He acts like nothing is wrong, but he's just waiting… waiting to see if he can have mother declared incompetent to run the business. Sean has heard he has a lawyer retained to see if he can gain control."

"What does Sean say about all of it?"

"He says that right now there is nothing Reilly can do. Mother is still in full control of her facilities but that was also one of the reasons it was important for you to come home. He'll explain it all to you. Just don't upset mother!"

When they entered the porch area Marlin got the first glimpse of his mother. She looked very thin and very frail but as she faced him and realized he was home, there was a sparkle in her eye. "It's about time you showed up around here!" she exclaimed as she rose from her rocker.

She hugged him tightly as if she would never let him go. She felt as small and fragile as she looked. "What's all this I hear about you being sick? You look fine to me," Marlin stated.

"Oh, I've been a little under the weather... nothing too serious, I'm fine. Just look at you... you're not my skinny little Marley any more you're a full grown man now! Sit down and tell me of your adventures. Tell me of your life at sea and life in Africa."

"How did you..."

"Marley, I'm your mother. I own the *Shamrock Isle* and I know Daniel Crowley. Just because I didn't infringe on your privacy doesn't mean I was going to sit here and worry about where you were and what you were doing. I would get reports now and then about where you were and what you were doing... nothing too detailed mind you, but enough to know you were alive and well... all a mother really needs to know. I knew you would have to leave and set off on your own at some point and, other than your father, there are no two better men to set off with then Captain Mike and Daniel Crowley. I imagine that in the process you learned a great deal about your father as well. He loved life on a ship almost as much as he loved hunting in Africa."

Marlin was surprised at first, but as he thought about it, it seemed to make sense. His mother wasn't the type to not have an answer to a question like, 'Where's my son?' Marlin knew now that his mother, sister and Sean Kilgore knew where he had been. Although he didn't want to upset her, he had to know, "What about George? Did he know where I was?"

His mother's eyes turned cold. It was a look in her eyes he had never seen. "No," she replied in a short empathic tone. "He has been told nothing of you or your whereabouts. It's none of his business!"

She looked directly into her son's eyes and went on, "Marley, we all make mistakes in life… bad decisions that we have to live with. Our character is based in part on how we choose to live our lives in spite of it all… how we carry on… what we learn from it."

While his mother never spoke of his decision to run away with Mary but he got the distinct impression she was addressing his poor decision as much as her own in marrying George. They both had made decisions in their lives they regretted. Decisions that would stay with them for the rest of their lives, but as Marlin had been learning, life would go forward and you still had to live your life.

At that point, Calvin came out on the porch, "Miss Ruth, can I bring some refreshments?"

Ruth Colby's tone changed immediately, "Yes indeed Calvin. Sally and I will have some lemonade and I would imagine my son would like some Irish whiskey… and Calvin, since this is a special occasion, please put a drop of the whiskey in my drink as well." Then she turned her attention back toward Marlin, "Now, please tell me of your adventures."

Marlin began the tale of his travels and his mother and sister sat spellbound. When he could see that his mother was beginning to tire, he stopped the story. "Would you like to rest for a while?" he asked.

"Yes. I usually take a short nap around this time each day. I'll see you at dinner," she replied before heading upstairs to her bedroom.

Sean Kilgore had come by to see Sally and was just beginning to sit down with Marlin to explain some things when George Reilly walked through the front door. George was used to seeing Sean in the house and while he now didn't particularly like him much, he knew he had to put up with him. He didn't recognize Marlin at first but as soon as he did, a sour look of disgust came over his face. "I see the bad seed has returned home," he said in a tone of arrogance and dislike.

Marlin stood up and George realized it wasn't the same person he had bullied in the past. He looked directly into George's eyes and in a very cool and confident tone replied, "I've come home to visit my mother, so let's try not to upset her."

George just grumbled something under his breath and wandered off to his room. He left the house about twenty minutes later giving Marlin a scowl as he left. Marlin knew there would be a confrontation with George but it wasn't time yet. He needed to make him uncomfortable. He needed to stir up some panic in George.

*Chapter 32*

# Plan of Action

"Marley, I've some information we need to talk about," Sean started. "First, we need to talk of your mother…"

"She seems so small and frail. What is exactly wrong?" asked Marlin.

"Simply put, it's just old age setting in. She has some medical issues… her heart is weak, but there is nothing wrong with her mind. The doctor has said that she will probably just go in her sleep when her heart just stops. Rest and taking things easy is the best medicine… your coming home helps a great deal."

"I realized quickly that she has known all along where I was," Marlin commented.

"Yes, I'm sorry about betraying your confidence, but the worry of not knowing would have damaged her health more than knowing. Fact is; she was excited to know what little she could find out. She still worried mind you, but knowing you were following in the path of your father with Captain Mike and Daniel Crowley was a comfort to her. She kept George in the dark… things have not been good between them. He is a cruel and heartless man."

"What has he been doing?"

"He has a room here but rarely sleeps here. He keeps a place downtown where his mistress resides. Occasionally, he eats here but on those nights your mother takes her meal in her room. He receives a salary from the company but has no authority or actually works. Your mother is embarrassed and ashamed of the situation but has chosen to keep up a front. Everyone in town is aware of the situation. George hasn't changed a bit. He still drinks and will brawl with anyone who disagrees with him."

"So who's running the business?" Marlin asked.

"Sally has taken over most of what your mother was doing… although George doesn't know that. She's really very good at business. He thinks Ruth is still calling all the shots. The fact is that in a way she is… she's just approving of what Sally is doing. I look over all the transactions and contracts to make sure everything is legal."

"What do you think George's plan is? He's got to have something in mind."

"George is not going to be happy you're back. Watch out for him, Marley. It's my belief he wants to wait until there is a point where he can declare your mother is unable to make sound decisions and try to take over the business. Ruth is aware she doesn't have much time left. She's had me draw up a new will and business transfer that leaves George with nothing but she would not let me take it before a judge until you returned home. Now that you're home we must do that as soon as possible."

"What does a judge have to do with it all?" Marlin questioned.

"Not just a judge… two doctors and a judge. Before the new will and other documents are signed off by the court, Ruth wants to make sure there are no loopholes. She wants to be certified as sane and competent in her decision making so if George tries anything he hits a brick wall. We'll talk about it over dinner… I doubt George will be here after seeing you. I'd like to have the doctors and the judge come by tomorrow. Legally, what's on file with the court would be okay even if your mother were to die in her sleep tonight. George might be able to legally get something as it stands now but when the new paperwork goes into effect, not only will he get nothing, it will be explained why he gets nothing and he'll have no recourse."

Ruth was in exceptionally good spirits at dinner. George wasn't there and she was so happy to have her son home that nothing else seemed to matter. Over dinner it was decided that the following day she would meet with her doctors and the judge, an old friend of the family, to finalize the papers she wanted prepared. Marlin felt a bit awkward about just arriving home and having his mother put her affairs in order.

"Marley," she began. "I know this might seem a bit sudden because you just arrived home, but this process has been waiting for a while now and it needs to be handled. We need to be practical about this... my medical outlook is not good and I know it. When the end comes, as it will for all of us, we should be prepared and assured we have done the responsible things that must be done."

"Mother, please," Sally started. "I can't bear to think of these things..."

"Sally, you above all, must be practical," Ruth insisted. "It will be you, Marley, and Sean who will see to it my wishes are fulfilled. I'm not afraid to die... it will be much easier being prepared."

Sean interjected, "It will all be done as you wish, but for now I'd like to bring up another topic... something that I've been looking into for a few weeks. This will be of particular interest to Marley."

Everyone directed their attention to Sean as he went on, "Several weeks ago I received a letter from a priest... Father Bernard. He was ministering to the sick in Florida when he was contacted by a terminally ill patient... a man by the name of Sam Wiggins."

Sean looked at Marlin, who didn't react to the name or show any special interest. "Wiggins was a man I interviewed briefly when Marley was involved in the auto accident. I was very interested in him and before the incident was resolved, I mentioned to him that I would have some questions for him in court. Shortly after that, he disappeared for a time... at least until we left St. Augustine and there was no threat of a trial or hearing. Father Bernard wrote me in an attempt to contact Marley because Wiggins had confessed on his death bed that he was drunk and responsible for the accident. In fact, he confessed that he had tried to pour liquor down Marley's throat, poured it on his person and stole his money."

Marlin became very uncomfortable. This was just as he feared it would be. He would come back and everything from his past would be dredged up again. "What good can this possibly do at this point?" he asked, now that the issue was in the forefront of conversation. "It won't bring Mary back."

"That's true," Sean continued. "But the truth needs to be told... your reputation and Mary's needs to be cleared. In hindsight, you would agree that you and Mary running off was a bad idea but you were both young at the time. Young people do foolish things but other than being foolish, the idea that you committed a crime or that you were drunk and responsible for her death should be addressed. Being in love and being foolish is not against the law."

Ruth was now very interested, "What do you propose to do with this information Sean?"

"I hope I have not stepped out of line, but I have arranged for Father Bernard to come here and talk with Marley. I want Marley to hear him out... hear Sam Wiggin's story. Wiggin's wanted to leave this world with a clear conscience... he wanted to make things right before he met his maker. Then I would like to have Father Bernard talk to the newspapers."

"I don't know...," Marlin started.

"I think that's a splendid plan!" Ruth exclaimed. "It won't be long before people in Charleston know Marley has come home and that will get their little tongues to wagging! Old issues and gossip will start again. George has brought enough shame on this family with his conduct. If Father Bernard has information that looks favorably on Marley then it should be brought out. People who dislike us for whatever reason will do so without cause, but fair minded people, they will weigh the facts. And you're right Marley, it won't bring Mary back, but don't you think she would want the truth to be told. She above all people would not want you to carry an unfair burden."

While not completely convinced, Marlin agreed to the meeting. He then asked, "And what about George? Do we address his conduct? Do we step in and deal with him?"

Ruth smiled a sly smile and looked over at Marlin, "Tomorrow we will deal with my husband. I made a very poor choice when I married him and I must apologize for that. If my religious beliefs were different, I would have divorced him long ago, but that was not an option. He hasn't taken to account that simple phrase that was part of the wedding vows… 'until death do you part'… something that is coming soon. When that time comes I will be reunited with your dear father and George will get a big surprise!"

*Chapter 33*

# Father Bernard

It was a week later when Father Bernard arrived in Charleston. Sean met him at the train station and got him situated in a fine hotel. By this time, Ruth's affairs had been put in order without George's knowledge. As expected, she had been declared in complete control of her faculties by two doctors and the judge had seen to it that all the paperwork had been approved by the court. George had come by the house a few times since Marlin's return. George took every opportunity to belittle, condemn or agitate Marlin… always making sure Ruth wasn't in earshot. Rarely would Marlin address George and when he did it was only to caution him about upsetting his mother. Marlin still had an underlying fear of George Reilly that remained from when he was a boy, but now things were somewhat different. The confrontations took on more of a sizing up of each other for what they each knew was coming. Sean and Sally had observed it all and could feel the tension building.

One evening when Sally and Sean were alone, she referred to George's conduct towards Marlin, "I don't know how he can take it! That man is such a monster!"

"I wouldn't worry too much. Your brother will eventually put him in his place and would venture to guess it won't be pretty. George can say what he will as long as he doesn't upset your mother. Marley knows her heart is weak. He's not going to do anything to George until she passes."

"Mother might feel better if he did something to him right now!"

"Relax, sweetheart. Your mother has taken Marley aside and spoken to him privately. He's doing just as she has asked."

Marlin and Sean went to the hotel to meet with Father Bernard. Marlin wasn't completely convinced this was the right thing to do but felt he should give the priest a fair chance. Father Bernard could feel that something wasn't right... that Marlin felt uncomfortable about the situation. After he related the story of Sam Wiggin's confession he began to ask Marlin some questions.

"It seems strange to me that you would get what most people would look upon as good news and be so conflicted in your feelings," Father Bernard began. "What troubles you about this news?"

"I don't know. It's hard to explain. Something still doesn't seem right about it."

"You still feel guilty?" asked the priest.

"Yes," replied Marlin. "I still feel very guilty."

"You should feel guilty," the priest continued. "I'm not here to abolish you of guilt, you have to take a certain amount of responsibility in the matter... but you must also understand that Mary would also have to take some responsibility. The decision to run away was made by both of you. You realize now it was foolish... had the accident never happened you both might have reached that conclusion and returned home but you never got that chance. The guilt you feel for having survived is normal. Why the Lord took her and not you is something beyond our ability to understand or comprehend. You must assume he allowed you to live for a reason."

Marlin sat in silence as Father Bernard continued, "This is a very unique situation. Normally a man's confession is kept in a sacred confidence but in this case, Sam Wiggins wanted your name cleared... he wanted to clear his conscience as well."

"What happens now?" Marlin asked.

Sean picked up the conversation at that point. "I would like Father Bernard to retell the story to the newspaper. Your mother was right in that the press will soon know you're in town. When she passes it will be a big event in this town. It would be good for her to know this matter is behind you for the most part... it will never be completely gone... people will always talk."

"I don't want to talk with the newspaper!" Marlin exclaimed.

"You won't have to. Father Bernard will do that. He will tell the story just as he told it to us... two young people made a bad decision and there was a tragic event... the truth."

"What about her parents?" Marlin asked.

"I think it's important for her parents to know the truth as well," the priest explained. "I will pay them a visit but don't expect miracles from them. They lost their daughter. Nothing can make that better. In time they may come to understand it wasn't your intent to harm her."

When the newspaper printed the story it was the talk of the town. It was a preemptive strike of sorts. The newspaper attempted to interview Marlin but he held them off. As they dug into what he had been doing in his time away, he became more interesting. The story of the accident drifted into the background and adventures on the high seas and Africa came to the forefront. Marlin soon learned that others would supply favorable stories of his time in Africa without him having to say a word. Eventually he did talk to some reporters who gained his trust but he would speak very little about the accident. He had the perfect excuse because he remembered very little of what happened. Most reporters were more interested in his African adventures and wanted to concentrate on that aspect of his life.

All of this attention infuriated George Reilly. He made a habit of getting drunk and besmirching anything positive said about Marlin. What he was saying would get back to Marlin, Sally and Sean. Captain Mike became so angry that he started to look for George so he could confront him but Sean got word of it and stopped him. In the meantime, Ruth's health was quickly fading. One night as dinner was just about finished she made a statement to her family just before retiring to bed.

"It's important for all of us to remember our place in life," she began. "We each arrive here naked and with nothing. No matter how rich or successful we become in this world, we can't take anything away with us into the next world... only the warmth of the love of those who have gone ahead of us or those we leave behind. We are only a small part of something much greater... it's important to live our lives honestly and with dignity."

Ruth Colby went to her room that night and knelt by her bed, praying as she had done every night since she was a child. She then removed all her clothing and took off her wedding ring, setting on the nightstand next to her bed. As she lay under her covers she drifted away in her sleep, leaving the world as she had entered it.

## Chapter 34

# Funeral

The funeral was a big event in Charleston since the family was prominent but it was also more than that. Ruth Colby had done a great deal for the City and was well respected. She was a dignified lady who had married the wrong man but stuck to her religious beliefs. Her husband however was reviled by most people. There was an undercurrent of morbid curiosity about what was going to happen. It was now very public knowledge that there was dislike between George Reilly and Marlin.

During the ceremony and mass Marlin was reverent and very calm. When the time came, he delivered the eulogy. George was in attendance trying to present himself as the grieving husband but keeping his distance from Marlin. Sally cried throughout most of the ceremony and leaned on Sean for support. The tension was thick and it seemed everyone knew something was going to happen.

There was the procession to the cemetery and Ruth was laid to rest. Afterward there was a full scale Irish wake where friends could express their condolences over a few drinks of whiskey. While people were polite towards George, it was clear he was held in contempt. During the ceremony and in all the conversations regarding Ruth, no one referred to her as *Ruth Reilly...* she was constantly referred to as *Ruth Colby.* She was even mentioned that way in the newspapers, although it was pointed out that she had remarried and George was mentioned. The crew from the *Shamrock Isle* was in attendance, including Pee Vee who was a favorite of Marlin's mother. George steered clear of the crew... especially Captain Mike. Many of the other ships crews and dock workers attended as well. It was an eclectic mix of the wealthy elite of Charleston society and the common people.

There had been a conversation before the funeral service that took place between Marlin and Calvin, the butler. As Sally was getting ready to go and waiting for Sean, Marlin took Calvin aside. "Calvin, can I have a minute with you," he asked.

Calvin had been very upset over Ruth's passing. He had been quiet and withdrawn. "Yes Mister Marley... what can I do for you?"

"Calvin, I have something very important for you to do. It was one of my mother's last requests... my sister and Sean know nothing about it... it's something she wanted only you and I to know about and take care of... mother thought it might be something you would enjoy."

"I don't understand Mister Marley... Miss Ruth is gone... I don't see how there be nothin' I could enjoy right now."

"This is something I know you'll enjoy," Marlin began. "I want you to see to it that all of George Reilly's possessions in this house are boxed up and up put out on the street. I don't want you to do it because you're family... I want you at the funeral with us. I want you to call some people in to do it, but everything of his must be out of this house before the funeral is over. Can you take care of that?"

For the first time since Ruth passed away a smile came over Calvin's face. "Ol' Mister George ain't gonna be happy 'bout this! He'll be pissed!"

"That's what I'm counting on Calvin. I want him pissed off... I want him good and pissed off."

Calvin started to laugh quietly, knowing that this was a secret between him and Marlin. "Mister Marley, I will be happy to do it."

"Oh yes, I almost forgot. Don't have them pack up his stuff neatly like he's going on a trip. No folding of clothes and such... just stuff it all in some boxes... and if you run out of boxes, just pile it in the street."

A big grin came over Calvin's face as he replied, "Yes sir!"

*Chapter 35*

# Face the Lion

In Marlin's mind his mother had passed from this world and into the next at the point she died. The funeral was for those that she left behind, in part to show their gratitude and respect, in part to say good bye, but unknown to all but Marlin, it was also Ruth Colby's intent to close the last chapter in her life. It was Ruth's idea and request that George be put out on the street as soon as she died. While she wanted him handled in that fashion, it was Marlin's intent to make sure he was humiliated in the process. He didn't intend the door to that last chapter to be closed gently... he intended it to be slammed in George's face.

George would think he would have the big house to himself and a great deal of money to go along with it. Maybe after a respectful time move his mistress in. It was time to make George panic.

About an hour before leaving the after services gathering, Marlin sought out Mick O'Malley, one of the reporter's he had done an interview with and took him aside. He chose this reporter carefully, knowing he could be trusted.

"Mick, I'd like to talk with you a moment, if I may."

"Sure, Mister Colby. What would you like to talk about?"

"Mick, we're long past that 'Mister Colby' stage... please call me Marlin. I just wanted to share some information with you... something your paper will be interested in."

Mick O'Malley perked up... partly due to his new found familiarity with Marlin and partly because he sensed a big story. Marlin went on, "I know it's no secret that there are bad feelings between my step-father and myself. My family and friends have not dealt with George to this point in respect for my mother and her health issues. I'm going to give you some information that only you will have... an exclusive you might say, but I'm also going to give you some information I would like you to spread around to everyone after my sister, Sean and I leave the party. Can I trust you with that?"

"Of course Marlin," replied Mick. "I'm flattered you would give me the exclusive. What information would you like spread around?"

"My mother was embarrassed and deeply ashamed of her husband's conduct. She knew of his affairs... his drunkenness... his brawling... but as you know; my mother was a very religious person. She regarded George as, I guess you might say, her cross to bear. My family has considerable wealth and my mother was determined that George was not going to be rewarded for his bad conduct after her death. I was instructed that immediately upon her death, George was to be removed from her home... in actuality, he is rarely there since he has a girlfriend in town. As of this time, all of his belongings have been removed from the residence and placed out on the street. That's the part of the story I would like you to casually spread around. You might want to send a photographer out to take a few photos as well."

"Okay... but what's the exclusive part?" O'Malley asked.

"While the will is not going to be officially read for a few days, I want you to know that George will get nothing from the estate. He has been receiving an allowance from my mother for years... his position at the company was a title only... he was never allowed to make any critical decisions... oh, and by the way, that position with the company and his allowance... it also ended upon my mother's death. He is left only the sum of one hundred dollars in the will with the suggestion that he use the money to move out of town. My assumption is that he also stole some money over the years so I expect he'll have a bit of drinking money left."

"Is this on the level?" O'Malley questioned. "If it is, he's in for a big surprise. You know, he's not going to take this well."

"I assure you that it's on the level. My mother went to great lengths to make sure the will is not contestable. As far as the surprise is concerned... I guess we'll just have to wait and see."

When the family arrived home, Sally and Sean were shocked to see the pile of belongings on the street. Captain Mike had come home with them and casually asked Marlin, "What's all this? A bit 'o spring cleanin'?"

"No," replied Marlin. "This was Calvin's and my doing. It was one of mother's last requests… she wanted that no good son of a bitch out of this house as soon as she passed."

Calvin stood with a wide grin on his face nodding his head with approval, then muttered, "That no good son of a bitch…"

Then Marlin commented to everyone, "I expect the press has already sent the photographer to take a picture of all this. I expect George will getting word of his eviction shortly."

Calvin started laughing and then commented, "Mister Marley, you sure knows how to pull the tiger's tail!"

"Not a tiger's tail… a lion's tail," replied Marlin in a calm voice. "Let's all go inside and wait for George."

The family went inside and Captain Mike poured himself a drink. He had a worried look on his face. "Marley," he began. "George is gonna be fightin' mad when he gets here. He'll be lookin' for trouble…"

"I'm expecting that."

"Marley… he's got about fifty pounds on you!" exclaimed Captain Mike. "Maybe ya best let me handle 'im."

"No," replied Marlin emphatically. "I don't want anyone else to step in. This has been coming for a long time."

"Okay, but let me give ya some words of advice. I seen him in fights many a time an' he will always do the same thing every time. He's got what ya call a rhythm… he always takes three punches with his right… then he tries to hit ya hard with his left. Watch out for that left… that's the one that'll git ya. The rights are just set ups… but they can hurt ya too. Give 'em his three rights then hit 'em hard before he can get the left in. Don't let 'em get ya in a bear hug… he'll squeeze the life out of ya… if he gits ya in a bear hug, stomp on his toes. Fight dirty, 'cause he will."

Marlin poured a glass of whiskey for himself and Captain Mike. As they raised their glasses they could hear the commotion of a crowd approaching the house. They raised their glasses to each other, downed the shots and Marlin stated, "Time to face the lion."

At that instant the front door burst open and George Reilly burst in, "What's all this I hear about you kickin' me outta my own home?"

Marlin looked at George. He was large, drunk, and angry. He had rage in his eyes but he didn't advance. "What you heard is true," Marlin answered, his voice unwavering. "I'm sure you noticed we took the liberty of packing for you."

With that, George started to advance on Marlin, "I'm gonna take great pleasure in beatin' you…"

There was a great deal of commotion inside the house for about a minute as things got knocked about. Sally let out a scream as Marlin punched George knocking him through the closed front door. The crowd standing in the street saw the front door knocked off its hinges and George tumble down the front steps. A moment later Marlin walked out the front door and looked down at George. The crowd started to cheer and the flashbulbs of the photographers went off. George jumped to his feet and landed a punch on Marlin who stumbled back, tripped and went down as the fight moved into the street. He followed up with a kick to Marlin's ribs then picked up a chair from the pile of his belongings and was just about to hit

Marlin over the head when he felt the barrel of a pistol at the back of his head.

Captain Mike pushed the gun a little harder just to make his point, "Don't be makin' me blow yer miserable brains all over these nice people. Now drop the chair... for once in yer life yer gonna have a fair fight."

Marlin had gotten to his feet by this time and gave a nod to the Captain that he was ready to proceed. George dropped the chair and put up his hands. It was just like Captain Mike said... three right punches and a swing with the left. Marlin got a punch in before he was hit with the left and George fell into the pile of his belongings. The crowd milled about as George struggled to get his feet under him. There were several people now placing bets on the fight and the police had arrived.

George was over confident and drunk and beginning to wear down. He started to swing wildly, missing most of his punches and getting out of his rhythm but the punches he was landing took a toll on Marlin. One eye was swollen almost shut and a blow to his ribs had cracked a bone but he continued the fight. He remembered Bwana Dan's advice to not panic and to think.

By coincidence, it was Captain Jones who arrived with the police. Jones had a dislike of George going back to the time when he delivered the news of the accident. Since that time he had caused enough trouble in town to make Captain Jones well aware of who he was. Sean was able to get to him before he got to the heart of the fight. "What's going on here?" Jones demanded.

"It's George Reilly Captain. He's fighting with Marlin Colby."

"George Reilly!" he exclaimed. "How's Colby doing? Is he holding his own?"

"He's giving Reilly more than he can handle," replied Sean.

"Do you think he'll be able to give him a good beating?"

"Captain, I think George Reilly is going to get all he deserves."

"Well," Jones answered. "It's my duty to keep the peace here… make sure all these people stay safe so I think the first thing we'll do is hold the crowd back so no one other than the two fighters gets hurt… that might take a while."

The police held the crowd back and the fight went on. George was finding that Marlin wasn't going to be the push over he thought he was. When he landed a punch to his mid- section it was like punching a rock and Marlin was now landing punches almost at will. George landed a lucky punch to Marlin's head and he stumbled. In an instant, he had him in a bear hug, trying to squeeze the life out of him. Marlin stomped down as hard as he could on George's foot and felt his grip release as he let out a scream.

Once out of his grip, Marlin faced George again. In that moment when they faced each other he looked into George's angry eyes. For a brief moment he was back in Africa staring into the eyes of the lion who had just killed Sironka. He was expecting to feel fear, but there was no fear, just contempt and his own anger. George moved in again but his punches were now weak, but he landed a punch to his nose. Suddenly Marlin felt the rage he had experienced all those years ago when George broke his nose and he left home. George threw three rights as a follow up but missed each time. Then Marlin hit him as hard as he could square on the nose before he could hit him with his left fist. George's nose was now bleeding heavily, he was still standing but swaying back and forth. Marlin hit him in the face again, releasing all the pent up rage he had been holding back for all those years. George's eyes rolled back, he swayed a bit and he fell to the ground. He was knocked out for a moment until someone threw a bucket of water on him. He laid there completely exhausted and thoroughly beaten as he looked up at Marlin.

Marlin stood over George and looked down at him. He was breathing heavily, bleeding and one eye was swollen shut. "I wouldn't get up if I were you... if you do, I plan to hit you even harder and put you down there again," Marlin stated. Then he took a one hundred dollar bill from his pocket and dropped it on George's chest. As he did so he proclaimed in a voice loud enough for all to hear, "My mother's will stipulates that you get one hundred dollars... it's all the money you'll get. She also suggested that you leave Charleston, but that's up to you... by the way, you're fired!"

Suddenly the crowd standing close to where George was lying on the ground started laughing. The people in the crowd had watched in amazement as Pee Vee strutted up on his short little legs through the crowd and proceeded to lift his leg and pee on the helpless George. The entire crowd was now roaring with laughter and cheering at seeing George Reilly get beat by Marlin and peed on by a little dog. The police disbursed the crowd and the Colby family went back into the house. George lay on the ground for a long while trying to get his breath back and figure out all that had happened. He finally got up after everyone left and slinked off alone. In the house, Calvin gathered up some cool water and towels and Sally started fusing over her brother, cleaning up his cuts as he sat in a comfortable chair. Captain Mike poured some whiskey for himself, Sean, Calvin, and of course, Marlin. Pee Vee sat looking up with his begging face on and Captain Mike couldn't refuse. "I guess any dog smart enough ta pee on George Reilly has earned a shot a whiskey." Then he looked over at Sally and asked, "Miss Sally, a small shot a whiskey for ya?"

The whole day had finally caught up with Sally... the funeral, the burial, all the people, the reporters and now the big fight. She looked up at Captain Mike, her future husband Sean, Calvin, Marley, even Pee Vee... they were all smiles and satisfaction over the outcome. Sally just sighed, laughed at the entire situation and said, "I guess Mom had a real Irish funeral... what the hell, pour me one, too."

Then Captain Mike made a toast before they downed the whiskey, "Somewhere up in heaven your mother and father are reunited an' smilin' down on all a us."

Marlin drank down his whiskey and couldn't help but think that somewhere a Maasai warrior named Sironka was looking down on him as well, knowing he had faced his lion.

# Epilog

Marlin stayed in Charleston long enough to help with the transfer of the shipping company operations to Sean and Sally. He would retain a level of ownership of the company but he was still restless. He wasn't ready to settle down to the life of a shipping magnate. Sean was well suited to the running of the operation and could be trusted. With Sally at his side they would pick up where his mother left off becoming a power couple in Charleston society. George hung around Charleston for a while, pleading his case about how he was cheated to anyone who would listen. Eventually he ran out of money and left, never to be heard from again. The rumor was he went to New Orleans where he was caught sleeping with a married Cuban woman. The husband took offense to this, so he shot George and killed him along with his wife before fleeing to Key West where he went to work in the cigar trade. The police in New Orleans eventually tracked him to

Key West but by that time he made it back to Cuba. They didn't spend much more time on the investigation figuring the murderer had left the country and reasoned George and his lover got what they deserved.

Marlin signed on to work on the *Emerald Isle* and headed back to Africa where his adventures continued.

# Aknowledgements

**Thanks to the following;**
Pamela Marchetti
William Bretz
Maasai Association
NRA/American Rifleman
Charleston Historical Society
St. Augustine Historical Society

# About the Author

Mark Marchetti was born and raised near San Jose, CA. He graduated from Los Altos High School and went on to earn degrees from De Anza College and California State University San Jose. He was involved in sports and music as a child and became a music instructor while still in high school. At seventeen his parents gave him perhaps the greatest gift of his life... SCUBA diving lessons. He has always been fascinated by the sea and spends a great deal of time diving or surfing. Diving has taken him all over the world exposing him to many of the exotic people and places he writes about. He has been a diving instructor and has done work as a commercial diver. He continues to travel and dive on a regular basis. Mark has always loved history and mixes historical facts with legends and fiction in his writing.

After college he began a twenty eight year career in law enforcement. He still teaches firearms training at the regional police academy. During his earlier years he also became interested in auto and motorcycle racing, participating in races for a few years. He still likes to cruise Highway one on his Harley Davidson, enjoying some of the most dramatic scenery in the world. Hunting, fishing and golf are also priorities in his life.

Mark has four adult children. He lives with his wife, Pamela, dividing their time between homes in Montara, California and Catalina Island.

Thanks for reading this book.
I hope you enjoyed the story.

Please visit our web site at;
lizardkeybook.com

Other books by Mark Marchetti
Lizard Key
Texas Jack
Black Bart's Treasure
Rocky the Rodeo Pony

Coming soon;
"Texas Jack" McKenna returns in
Scalp Hunters